JESSE OWENS

Illustrated by Meryl Henderson

JESSE OWENS
Young Record Breaker

by M. M. Eboch

ALADDIN PAPERBACKS

New York   London   Toronto   Sydney

For anyone who refuses to give up

❦

ALADDIN PAPERBACKS
An imprint of Simon & Schuster Children's Publishing Division
1230 Avenue of the Americas, New York, NY 10020
Text copyright © 2008 by Chris Eboch
Illustrations copyright © 2008 by Meryl Henderson
All rights reserved, including the right of reproduction
in whole or in part in any form.
ALADDIN PAPERBACKS and related logo are
registered trademarks of Simon & Schuster, Inc.
CHILDHOOD OF FAMOUS AMERICANS is a
registered trademark of Simon & Schuster, Inc.
Designed by Christopher Grassi
The text of this book was set in New Caledonia.
Manufactured in the United States of America
First Aladdin Paperbacks edition January 2008
2 4 6 8 10 9 7 5 3 1
Library of Congress Control Number 2007924838
ISBN-13: 978-1-4169-3922-1
ISBN-10: 1-4169-3922-9

ILLUSTRATIONS

CONTENTS

JESSE OWENS

Saving J. C.

James Cleveland Owens woke up in the dark. He could hear his family stirring. Soon, Mama would make breakfast. He lay in the dark and rubbed his chest. He felt a bump, and it was sore. J. C. sighed, remembering the day before September 12, 1918—his fifth birthday. They didn't have money for presents in the Owens household, but a birthday was still special. It was one of the few days they got to eat meat during the week. Yesterday it was ham. Everyone made a fuss about J. C. since he was the baby of the family. It was fun.

J. C. jumped out of bed and pulled on his pants. By the time Mama put corn bread in front of him, he'd forgotten about the bump.

He couldn't forget for long, though. The bump kept growing and hurting. As it grew out it also seemed to press in on his chest. Jesse told Mama, but there wasn't much she could do. The nearest doctor to Oakville, Alabama, was seventy-five miles away, in Birmingham. But it hardly mattered. The family didn't have any money for a doctor.

A month later, J. C. could barely breathe with the pressure on his chest. He wondered if he would die. He lay down, gasping, unable to sleep. He heard his parents whispering.

"We've got to do something, Henry," his mother said.

"You took one of those bumps off his leg once."

"But this one's so big!" Mama said. "And it's near his heart."

"Emma—" his father started to say.

"Don't say it!"

"I'm going to say it," his father insisted. "If the Lord wants him—"

His mother interrupted again, her voice rising. "The Lord doesn't want this child."

Three of her babies had died at birth. Ten had lived, though two more would die young. Some would say Emma Owens was lucky that so many of her children had survived. In those days, many poor families lost more than half of their children at birth or in early childhood, and mothers often died giving birth without a doctor's care.

But Emma couldn't bear the thought of losing her child. Young J. C. had a special place in her heart. She'd had him when she was in her late thirties and thought she was too old to have more children. She called James Cleveland her "gift child."

J. C. finally fell asleep. Sometime later, his mother shook him awake. It was still dark out. J. C. looked around to see all his brothers and sisters awake and watching. A few of them tried to smile at him, but he could tell by their eyes that they were worried.

His mother picked up a knife and held it in the fire until the blade seemed to glow. She walked over to J. C. and looked straight into his eyes. "I'm going to take off the bump now, J. C.," she said.

He felt the knife going into his skin. It went around and around as his mother tried to cut the thing loose. J. C. had felt pain before. It had hurt when his mother took the bump off his leg. Every winter, he got sick with what they called the devil's cold. The coughing and burning fever nearly killed him. And once he got caught in an animal trap his father had set. But this was much worse.

J. C. saw tears running down his father's face. He heard a voice that sounded far away. "Aww, Mama, no . . ." He realized it was his own voice.

Finally he blacked out.

When he woke up, it was still dark. J. C. didn't even know if it was the same night or the next. Everyone was still in the house. J. C. could tell from their clothes that they hadn't been to the fields. The only time no one went to work was on Christmas Day—or when someone died.

J. C. knew he must be dying.

He tried to speak, but couldn't. The family gathered around.

"I got it all out," his mother said softly. "All of it."

But there were tears in her eyes. She pressed a crop bag against J. C.'s chest. The blood quickly soaked through that one. She replaced it with another. J. C. kept bleeding.

They couldn't wash and dry the bags quickly enough. When they ran out of crop bags, they used rags. Then they used pieces of their clothing. The bleeding went on all night.

In the morning, J. C.'s father and brothers had to go work in the fields. His mother stayed by him, mopping up blood and praying. Finally she fell into an exhausted sleep beside him. J. C. watched in horror as his blood soaked into her shirt.

J. C. tried to stay awake, but he kept passing out. Every time he woke up, his first thought was, *Am I still bleeding?* He always was. How much blood could he have left?

J. C. woke to find the house dark and his mother asleep again at his side. J. C. heard a faint voice that sounded miles away. He tried to lift himself and got up on one elbow. It was a dark, moonless night, and he couldn't see anything.

He sat up, trembling with weakness. He could still feel the blood trickling down his chest. But now he could hear his father's words.

"She'll die."

What could that mean? J. C. stumbled toward the voice. It was coming from just outside the front door.

"Oh, Lord Jesus," his father went on. "Please hear me. This saving means everything. She'll die if he dies. And if she dies, Lord, we'll all die—all of us."

J. C. crawled to the doorway. He could feel his blood coming in spurts, and knew that he hardly had any left. He felt a glowing kind of haziness. It scared him more than he'd ever been scared before. His head spun, but he dug his fingernails into the wood floor. He pulled himself toward the open doorway. Outside, his father was on his knees, praying.

"She'll die if you take him from me. She always said he was born special. Please don't take him from me, Lord. I'll do anything— the hardest thing—to pay you back."

J. C. must have made a noise. His father turned to him, still kneeling, and reached out. "J. C.!" Even in the black night, J. C. somehow felt his father's eyes looking into his own. "Pray, J. C.," his father said. "Pray, James Cleveland."

J. C. cleared his throat. "What should I say, Daddy?"

"I don't know, J. C., just pray."

They knelt together, side by side, and prayed. Finally, J. C.'s father lifted him in his arms and carried him back into the house. The bleeding had stopped.

In the morning, J. C. could sit up easily. By dinnertime, he was eating like a mule. The following day, he could walk around. By the weekend, he was helping in the fields.

"He may be sickly in body," J. C.'s father said, "but our boy has a strong spirit. If he survived that pain, he'll survive anything life has to offer. Pain won't mean nothing to him now."

A Fight

J. C.'s father, Henry Owens, was the son of
former slaves. He had nothing but his shack,
a mule, and his work as a sharecropper. He
worked for the white man who owned the
land. Henry plowed, planted, and harvested
the crops. Then he kept half, and gave the
other half to his landlord. That was the way
people lived all through the South.

Growing food meant hard work. Even the
children helped in the field. In the spring
they ran a plow behind the mule, and planted
cotton and corn in the fields. Beans, onions,

tomatoes, and squash grew in the family garden. They had to be planted and picked as well.

Once the crops were in the ground, the boys could sometimes steal a few hours for fun. One hot morning, they headed off to the local swimming hole. J. C. ran ahead, his thin legs pumping. His tough bare feet slapped the ground. He sucked in the hot, humid air, feeling his lungs strain. He felt like he could run anywhere. Running made him feel free.

J. C. saw the sparkle of water ahead. He let out a whoop and ran faster. He leaped from the bank and flew out over the water. His splash sent the water spraying. Neighbor boys, both black and white, laughed and shouted. One of them swam to J. C. and dunked him playfully.

J. C.'s brothers tumbled in after him. They splashed and swam and wrestled in the mud. The cool water felt wonderful. Maybe later they would go possum hunting. Maybe they would camp around a fire that night, the boys and their dogs. On a day like that, they could forget the cold winds of winter. They could forget the hard work of planting. They could forget the cotton harvest that was coming. Life was simple, and good.

Finally, the boys crawled to the bank and settled under the oak trees. J. C.'s brothers and some of the other boys started fishing. They used string, with hooks made from bits of scrap metal. If they were lucky, they might bring a fish or two home for dinner. If not, they would enjoy the lazy afternoon, anyway.

They sprawled along the edge of the pond, boasting and teasing one another. But J. C. didn't feel like fishing. He prowled about, picking up stones and tossing them into the water.

"You'll scare the fish," a boy grumbled, just as if they hadn't all been splashing around a few minutes before.

"What's up, J. C.?" his brother Prentice asked. "Can't you sit still for a minute?"

J. C. grinned and shook his head. How could he sit still, when it felt so good to move?

He trotted away from the lake, not caring where he was going. He knew this part of Alabama too well to get lost. He knew the farms and the woods. He knew his neighbors. He knew the little town where he went to school when he didn't have to work in the fields.

J. C.'s feet took him across a little bridge. He stopped and gazed up at a large white house. This was where his daddy's boss lived. It was hard to imagine people needing so much room. J. C. had only seen a few houses like that. All of them belonged to rich white people.

Many of his neighbors were white. But white or black, they were mostly poor. Only a few white people owned the land and had money. Everyone else worked for those landowners. J. C. didn't really care. He had his family, and they had enough to eat. He didn't miss what he had never had. And he remembered his daddy's advice: "No matter how hungry you ever get, J. C., and no matter how much the man next door has in his cupboard, don't let yourself envy him. And don't ever let yourself hate him either."

J. C. heard a shout. He turned to see one of the landowner's sons, Lawrence Cannon.

"What are you looking at?" Lawrence said.

"Nothing," J. C. said. "I was just looking." He smiled. His father had told him, always smile when you talk to white people. Be careful what you say. If they take offense, you could be in real trouble. Be polite and be careful.

This boy was J. C.'s age, but J. C. didn't know him well. Rich white children didn't play with poor black children. They didn't go to the same school either. J. C.'s school was only for black children.

Still, J. C. thought he could be friends with anyone. Why not?

Lawrence stepped closer and laughed. "Look at you, in those rags. You don't even have enough clothes to cover your dirty body."

J. C. looked down at himself. It was true, his clothes were ragged. His shirt had been handed down from brother to brother, all the way down to J. C. It had been torn and mended a hundred times. The wet shirt stuck to J. C.'s skin as it dried. The cloth was so thin, you could practically see through it.

J. C.'s smile wavered as he looked at Lawrence's clothes. He had a shirt with buttons up the front. The buttons were all the same. The shirt didn't look like it had ever been mended. It was too new. The boy had pants that reached all the way down to his ankles, and didn't have holes in the knees. He even had shiny dark shoes.

Still, J. C. tried to do what his father always told him. "You sure do have nice clothes," he said. "I wish I had clothes like that."

Lawrence laughed long and loud. He turned away and said, "Did you hear that? This dirty little cotton picker wants clothes like mine."

J. C. hadn't seen the girls sitting under a tree. One was Lawrence's sister, and the other was a neighbor girl. They were dressed in long, pretty dresses and had ribbons in their hair. J. C. burned with shame as they glanced at him and giggled.

"I'll have nice clothes someday!" J. C. insisted. "You'll see."

Lawrence turned back to him with a sneer. "You'll never have anything. You will always be a poor piece of dirt. Just like your daddy and your mama."

J. C.'s smile was gone now. "Don't you say bad things about my mama."

The boy took a step closer. He was a little taller than J. C., and a lot heavier. "And what are you going to do about it? Your mama ain't nothing but a—"

J. C. didn't wait for Lawrence to finish.

He threw himself at the boy. "You keep your mouth shut!"

Lawrence fell backward, with J. C. on top of him. Lawrence yelled, but J. C. didn't hear what he said. He was too mad.

Hands grabbed J. C.'s arms and pulled him up. They held him off the ground so his feet kicked the air.

J. C. looked right and left and saw Lawrence's older brothers. He twisted and kicked, but he couldn't get free.

Lawrence stood up and brushed off his clothes. "Now you'll pay," he said. "I'll cut my initials in your face."

J. C. blinked, trying not to cry. He couldn't think what to do. His father's advice came back to him, but it was too late. He couldn't think of any words to make these mean boys let him go. He couldn't even make himself say he was sorry.

"Hold him," Lawrence said, "while I get a knife."

J. C. squirmed. The hands dug into his arms.

J. C. took a deep breath, and suddenly felt calm. He remembered something else his daddy had said. Pain wouldn't bother J. C., not since the time Mama cut off the bump. No matter what they did to him, he wouldn't cry or scream. He would keep smiling, even if they hurt him. They might bruise his body or cut his face. But they couldn't kill his spirit.

J. C. heard a shout and the pounding of running feet. He craned his head to look back over his shoulder. His brothers were running toward him.

The hands let go, and J. C. dropped to the ground. He landed on his knees in the dirt. He scrambled to his feet as his brothers thundered up to him.

They stopped, gasping for breath. "You okay?" Prentice asked.

J. C. nodded. He turned to see the white boys running up to their house.

Quincy said, "Let's get out of here."

They ran back across the bridge and didn't stop until they were outside their house.

"How did it happen?" Prentice asked.

J. C. looked down at his feet. "Lawrence laughed at my clothes. Two girls were watching."

Prentice patted J. C.'s shoulder. "He was just showing off, I bet. But we showed them."

J. C. glanced back toward the big house. "What will they do?"

His brothers looked at each other. Prentice said, "Probably nothing. They won't tell, if they could get in trouble too. And Mr. Cannon is fair enough. But you keep your distance for a while."

Quincy said, "It never does any good to fight with white people. They always win."

Prentice scowled. "You sound like Pop. Sometimes you have to fight."

"Didn't you hear?" Quincy said. "Just last week, a man was arrested in Decatur. They said he insulted a white woman. He didn't do nothing but try to sell her some vegetables. But who will believe him?"

Prentice's shoulders slumped. "I know. Sometimes it seems like we can never get ahead. But there's got to be more to life than this." He straightened. "Someday I'd like to own my own land. My own, so no one can tell me what to do with it."

"They say it's better in the North," Sylvester said. "A man can get a job in a factory. He can make real money. Wear a suit, and shiny shoes, and a hat. Maybe even buy an automobile."

The boys fell silent as they thought of that. Only a few rich people owned cars. It was hard to imagine having that much money.

Finally Prentice said, "Maybe someday we'll find out." He slapped J. C. on the back. "Don't tell Mama what happened. She'd just worry."

J. C. nodded, and went inside. His mother stood by the stove, running an iron over a pair of pants. A basket of clean laundry sat at her feet.

These clothes didn't belong to the Owens family. J. C.'s mother washed and ironed other people's clothes for money. J. C. watched his mother as sweat ran down her face and darkened the back of her old dress. It was hot in the shack, but she had to stand by the stove while she worked.

She put the iron back on the stove to stay hot, and neatly folded the pants. She glanced at J. C. and smiled. "What kind of trouble have you been getting into?"

J. C. looked down and rubbed a bare toe across the floor. "Nothing. I just been looking around."

"Well you be careful now. You look hard enough for the devil, and the devil'll find you." Mama picked up a dress from the basket.

J. C. stared at the frilly dress. He remembered the way the girls had giggled. His face burned with the memory.

He walked over to his mother. "Mama, someday I'm going to have a nice suit of clothes."

She smiled down at him. "I bet you will, baby."

"I'll buy you a nice dress too," J. C. went on. "We'll all have nice clothes, and maybe even an automobile." He squared his shoulders. "Someday, I'm going to be somebody."

His mother put down the iron. She gathered him in her arms and hugged him tight. "I know you will, baby. You already are."

The Hardest Thing

J. C. kept away from the big house for a few weeks. He quickly forgot about the trouble with Lawrence. He didn't know how to hold a grudge.

Summer led to harvest season. J. C. joined his father and brothers in the fields. They picked corn, sorghum cane, and cotton. Corn went to feed people and animals, while cane made molasses. Cotton made money for the landowner. It was the worst to pick. Cotton grew low, so adults had to either bend over to pick it or move down the row on their knees.

J. C. was shorter, so he didn't have to bend over. But the thorns scratched his hands until they bled. He didn't yet have thick, tough calluses covering his hands, like his father.

Harvest season brought rewards too, like fresh fruit. The boys picked apples, peaches, and pears by the bushel. J. C. was too small to reach most of the branches from the ground, but he could shimmy up the tree trunks. He climbed as high as he could, then straddled a branch. He dropped most of the fruit down to his brothers, but the juiciest piece he ate right there in the tree.

Back home, Mama and the girls worked over the hot stove. They canned fruit and vegetables from the garden for winter.

It was a busy time of year, but fun, too. J. C. liked seeing all the jars of colorful fruit and vegetables. It seemed like they had enough food to last forever. In the autumn, Daddy would slaughter a hog and smoke the meat. J. C.'s mouth watered thinking of the ham, ribs, and gravy.

On Sunday, they put aside work and went to the Oakville Missionary Baptist Church. The whole family dressed in their best clothes. For once, J. C. could feel proud. His best clothes were still hand-me-downs and had been mended many times. But at least he had enough to cover his body. He felt almost like a grown-up.

The family walked together down the dusty road. J. C. ran ahead, of course. He wouldn't be able to sit still during the sermon, if he didn't get the running out of his legs first.

They reached a small, unpainted building. It was both school and church to the black community. The family piled inside, greeting friends and neighbors. J. C.'s father was a deacon, so he went to help the preacher.

Everyone settled down and turned their attention to the preacher. J. C. sat up straight on the edge of his chair. He liked listening to the preacher, with his voice like music. Sometimes he spoke softly, and sometimes he thundered. The words seemed to roll around the room. It was like hearing a wonderful story-teller.

J. C. listened and sometimes mouthed the words after the preacher. He imagined stand-ing up and talking like that. People would hang on to his every word, gasping with sur-prise or delight. Someday he would be some-body, and people would listen to him speak.

He glanced at Mama. She smiled back at him and squeezed his hand.

After church, everyone filed outside, talk-ing and laughing. Mama shook hands with the preacher, and told him how much she'd enjoyed the sermon. J. C. wanted to do the same, but instead he just smiled shyly at the man. The preacher patted his head and said, "You're growing up into a fine young man, aren't you?"

Mama said, "He sure is. He'll make us proud one day."

J. C. grinned and ran off to play with the

other children. The men and older boys ran footraces, hollering and laughing. J. C. watched for a few minutes. His father was one of the fastest. His oldest brother, Prentice, was fast too. He was also the star pitcher of the Oakville baseball team. J. C. thought maybe he'd be able to race like them one day.

He started a game of tag with the other children. His cousin Mattie watched from the side, grinning. Finally, she called out, "It's no use playing with J. C.! You never can catch him."

Finally, everyone headed home for their big Sunday supper. J. C. trailed after his family, looking for anything interesting in the dry grass.

He heard his mama say, "Roy Taylor is heading north."

"Is that right?" said Daddy.

"He got a letter from his cousin up there," Mama said. "He's working in a steel mill. Says there's lots of work up North. Lots of opportunities for folks like us."

J. C. crept closer to listen.

Daddy shook his head. "My father and grandfather worked the land here. We've always been here. This is where we belong."

"Your father was born a slave," Mama snapped. "It don't do no good to keep acting like you're a slave too." She put her hand on Daddy's arm and said more gently, "It would be good for the boys to have a chance at something more."

Daddy said, "It don't profit a man none if he gets the whole world but loses what's inside himself."

"What's wrong with getting a good job?" Mama asked. "What's wrong with sending the boys to high school? They are good boys, and always will be. Why can't they have a nice future too?"

They were quiet for awhile. J. C. slipped between them. "Mama? Daddy? One of the boys told me about a place far away. It's called . . ." He thought for a minute, trying to get the word right. "College. Jimmy said at college you can become anything in the world you want to be. I'd like to go there."

Mama chuckled and gave him a playful tug on the ear. "James Cleveland Owens! Where in the world do you get your ideas? You are the one!"

"The crazy one," added Daddy, laughing.

J. C. laughed too, though he didn't know what was so funny. "Haven't you ever heard of college?"

Daddy shook his head again. "College is for white folks, not for us." He looked down at J. C. "It don't do a colored man no good to get himself too high. 'Cause it's a heck of a drop back to the bottom."

But Mama pulled J. C. close to her side. "You keep on dreaming, baby. What you put into life is exactly what you get out."

J. C. thought about that. He'd like to go to college, where you could become anything you wanted. He wasn't sure what he wanted, but he wanted to do something good. Maybe at college he could figure out what he should be.

Over the next few weeks, Mama kept talking about going north. Daddy was dead set against it, but most of J. C.'s brothers wanted to go. "I'll get there someday," Sylvester insisted. "Just you wait and see."

Then they got a letter from Lillie, one of J. C.'s older sisters. Lillie had moved to Cleveland, Ohio, a few years before. She'd found a job and a husband.

Sylvester read the letter aloud. He was the best reader. Their parents couldn't read at all. "I never knew you could make so much money," Sylvester read. "I never even dreamed it in Oakville. Y'all should come up here and join me. Life is better in Cleveland."

That set the family arguing again. J. C. wasn't sure what all the fuss was about. He asked Prentice, "What's the North like?"

Prentice stared into the distance for a minute. "They say it's like Paradise. You don't have to work in the fields there. You don't even have to see fields. You don't ever have to look at a cotton field again."

J. C. tried to imagine this. "If there aren't fields, what is there? Woods?"

Prentice laughed. "No fields and no woods. Just buildings as far as you can see. Tall buildings that rise up to the sky."

"Like Mr. Cannon's house?" The landowner's house had two stories. J. C. had never been inside, but he had seen the second-floor windows. It was strange to think about being up in the air like that, with people in the rooms below you.

"Even bigger," Prentice said. "Maybe five or six stories, one on top of the other."

"Won't they fall down?" J. C. asked.

"No. Everything is different in the big city. It's like magic." Prentice grinned at J. C.

"But what do you do if you don't work in the fields?"

"You work in a factory, making something,

like cars. Or you work in a shop. Even a colored man can work in a shop in the North. Maybe a store that sells food."

J. C. screwed up his face in thought. "You have to get food from a store? All of it? What about the garden?"

Prentice shook his head. "You might not have a garden. You might live in the top of one of those big buildings, with other buildings all around. No place for a garden. You work in a factory or a store, and you buy your food."

He gave J. C. a playful push. "But you, youngster, would go to school."

J. C. frowned. He didn't care much for school. The teacher always wanted him to sit still. And they just did the same thing every year, writing out the alphabet, and listening to the teacher read from books.

Prentice sighed. "But Daddy won't go," he whispered. "He's too scared."

J. C. thought about tall buildings, and no

fields, and school. Maybe Daddy was right about the North. Then J. C. remembered college. Was college in the North? Would J. C. be able to go, even though he wasn't white? He didn't want to work in the fields all his life, planting crops for someone else. That was no way to become somebody. Maybe Mama was right about the North after all.

That night, J. C. woke up and heard his parents talking softly.

"We have to go north," Mama said. "Otherwise, the boys will go without us, one after the other. They won't stay here forever. Do you want to be here all alone?"

"But what would I do in Cleveland?" Daddy asked. "We'd never make it, Emma. We'd starve."

"We're nearly starving here!" Mama exclaimed. "It's crazy to go on like this. The boll weevil destroys the cotton crops. We get too much rain, or not enough. We can never get ahead. And now they're making machines to do a farmer's work. What happens if Jim Cannon decides a machine can do the work better than you?"

"But how can we go?" Daddy asked. "It costs money to get there, and we don't have any."

"Sell something," Mama said.

"But what? Mr. Cannon owns the house, the land, the tools—everything."

"He doesn't own the mule," Mama said. "Sell the mule, and let's go north. You won't need a mule to plow the fields up there."

At last, Henry Owens agreed. He would do the hardest thing on earth for him. He would leave the only home he ever knew, so J. C. and the other children could have a better life.

The Colored Car

A few weeks later, Mr. Owens and his two oldest sons, Prentice and Quincy, were getting ready to leave Alabama. "Mama," J. C. said, "what's gonna happen?"

She pulled him close. "Daddy and Prentice and Quincy are going north. They'll find work, and then send for us."

"How will we get there?"

"We'll go on a train," Mama said.

"And where's the train gonna take us, Mama?"

"It's gonna take us to a better life."

She wrapped some bread in a piece of cloth. "Now you take this to Daddy. Them boys will get hungry on the train."

J. C. took the bread and ran to his father. Mr. Owens turned and bumped into J. C. "Whoa!" he said, grabbing J. C.'s arms to steady him. As he drew away, J. C. saw that his father's hands were shaking.

He really is scared, J. C. thought. Just like Prentice said. *I wonder what's so scary about the North. Everyone else says it's wonderful.* He figured he'd find out soon.

J. C. waved to his father and brothers as they walked away down the dusty road. He turned to see his mother wipe a tear from her eye. "All right, J. C.," she said. "There's work to be done. Idle hands are the devil's tool."

Work kept J. C.'s hands busy, but his mind still thought and thought about the future.

The next few weeks passed slowly. It seemed quiet without Prentice and Quincy around.

Had they found work yet? Had they seen those tall buildings? When would they send for the rest of the family?

Finally, the letter came. Prentice wrote, "We got jobs in the steel mill. We got a house to rent. Come soon." He sent money enough for the train ride for all of them.

Then they were busier than ever. They didn't own much, but Mama didn't want to leave anything behind. She just had to take all the canned fruits and vegetables they could carry, and even the scraps of cloth that weren't good for anything but rags. She picked every last bean and tomato from the garden. What they couldn't eat before they left, they gave to neighbors. "It don't do no good to waste," Mama said.

Finally they were ready. They put on their best clothes, the ones they wore to church. A neighbor came with his wagon to give them a ride to the train station. J. C. looked at the bundles piled on the wagon. He never realized they owned so many things.

J. C. climbed up after the bundles, along with Sylvester and his older sisters, Ida and Josephine. Mama sat up front, next to their neighbor. J. C. stared at their house as the wagon rolled away. It felt funny to think that he might never see it again. He would miss the little house, and the fields, and the swimming hole. Would they have a swimming hole in Cleveland? If they didn't have fields or woods, maybe they didn't have ponds, either. J. C. hadn't thought about that. What would the boys do on a hot summer day if they couldn't go swimming?

He turned to ask Mama, but she was staring back at the house. She blinked fast, and her eyes looked wet. Was she crying? Mama hardly ever cried. It scared J. C. But he leaned forward and touched her arm.

"We're going to a better life, Mama," J. C. said.

She took a fast breath and smiled down at him. "That's right, baby. We're going to a better life."

J. C. forgot his questions and worries as soon as they got to the train station. He had never been on a train before and he could hardly wait, but the train wasn't there yet. They went into the station, through the door marked COLORED.

Inside, J. C. looked all around. There was one counter where someone was selling tickets to white people, and another counter where someone was selling tickets to black people. Mama gave their money to Ida, and she went to buy the tickets. Mama sat on a bench, but J. C. and Sylvester went out to the platform to watch for the train.

"Here it comes!" a man yelled.

J. C. stared down the tracks. He could see puffs of smoke in the distance. He heard a faint rumble, and then the train's whistle blasted. The puffs got closer and bigger. The rumble got louder. J. C. backed away from the tracks, until he backed up against the building. He put his hands over his ears as the train's wheels screeched. He'd never heard such a noise. Coal dust billowed through the air and made him cough.

Finally the locomotive came to a stop. The engine in front was long, black, and shiny. Behind it, the train cars seemed to stretch forever.

"Will you look at that?" Sylvester said. "I bet you could put all of Oakville on that train."

J. C. could see faces through the windows. "Are all those people going to Cleveland?"

A man heard him and turned to answer. "No, son, they're going all over the country. This train will meet up with other trains going to other places. But if you want to get to Cleveland, you'd better get on board!"

"J. C.! Sylvester!" Mama called. "Get in here and help me." They ran inside and started picking up bundles. Then they went out and found the right train car, one with a COLORED sign above the door.

A porter greeted them. He was a black man

wearing a dark jacket with buttons all the way up the front. J. C. had hardly ever seen a black man dressed that nice, except the preacher on Sundays. The porter helped them into the car. They had to step up on a box, and then up into the tall train.

An aisle ran down the middle of the car, with benches on each side. They found seats and stowed all their bags on the racks above the seats. Then J. C. and Sylvester ran up and down the car, looking at everything.

The train started moving. J. C. grabbed on to a seat and held tight. His body shook right along with the train. The floor moved under his feet. He had never felt anything like it! He crawled across an empty seat to a window and stared out. The land outside flashed by, faster and faster. J. C. felt sick seeing the ground moving like that.

He sat back, closed his eyes, and took a deep breath. He told himself that the ground wasn't really moving. They were moving, on the train. When he felt better, he opened his eyes again.

J. C. couldn't sit still for long. He ran to the front of the car. It was a funny feeling, running on a floor that moved. He could feel the shaking every time his feet hit the wood.

There was a door at the front of the car. J. C. wondered where it led. He pressed his face against the glass. Sylvester came up beside him and did the same.

The porter smiled at them from the other side and opened the door. "This your first time on a train?" he asked.

"Yes, sir," J. C. said shyly.

"Then I reckon y'all want to see the front cars," the man said.

"Yes, sir!" the boys said together.

He led them through another car like theirs. Most of the seats were filled. Some folks had nice clothes, while others looked just as poor as the Owens family. All of them were black.

They went through to another car. The porter said, "Now here's our post office."

"A post office, right on the train?" Sylvester exclaimed.

"That's right. These men are employees of the U.S. Postal Department." He gestured toward four white men. One of them grinned and waved. Another was busy with a sack full of mail. He pulled out letters and tossed them into sorting bins. The porter said, "Those big bins are for mail going to big cities. The small bins are for small towns that we pass through. The railroads take mail all over the country."

J. C. wondered if the letters from Prentice and Lillie had come by train. He'd never thought about it before.

"Come through here and you'll get a real sight," the porter said. He led them through to another car.

This car was hot and smoky. Two men worked by something that looked like a big stove. The porter yelled over the noise, "That's the fireman and the engineer. They make sure the boiler has enough coal. They control the steam so the train has enough speed. That's what makes the train go."

One of the men picked up a scoop and shoveled more coal into the firebox. He had his sleeves rolled up, and his face shone with sweat.

The porter said, "They're busy. We'd best stay out of the way. There's nothing ahead besides the engine, anyway." He led the way back through the mail car to the passenger car.

"And what's behind us?" Sylvester asked. "Is it all more cars like ours?"

"Not all," the man said. "Behind these Jim Crow cars, they put the cars for white folks. They're in the back, so they don't get so much smoke from the engine. Then there's the dining car. It's like a restaurant."

"What do you mean," Sylvester asked, "you can buy food on the train?"

"That's right. They have tables, with white tablecloths, and men like me to serve the food. It's right fancy. But expensive. Mostly rich folks eat there, and the rest of us bring our own food."

J. C. thought the porter was nice. He didn't look down at them because they were poor, with ragged clothes. He treated the boys almost like grown-ups.

The man went on. "Behind the dining car, you have the sleeping cars. They have seats that turn into beds at night."

J. C. stared at him. "You could live on this train for a whole year!"

He laughed. "Some of us do, son. Some of us do. Now you boys run along. I'd better get back to work."

The train was the neatest place J. C. had ever been. He felt like he could stay there for days and days. He could watch the world go by outside the window and see all the different people who got on and off. "Maybe I'll be a train porter someday," he told Sylvester. "Then I could go all over the country. And I could have a nice suit!"

Sylvester nodded. "It must be about the best thing in the world, to be a porter."

Finally J. C. went back to his mother. She was staring out the train window as the fields went flying by. When J. C. sat next to her, she turned and pulled him close to her side. "Hungry, baby?"

J. C. nodded. Mama got out some bread and apples. Sylvester and the girls gathered around, and they all ate. J. C. thought about the dining car in the back. He imagined a man like the porter bringing him fancy food. Maybe even a steak! Only rich people ate steak. But J. C. was happier right there with his family, curled up against his mother's side.

J. C. fell asleep for a while. He woke up when the train came to a stop, and he crawled over his mother's lap so he could see out the window. This train station was bigger than the last one. It had a long brick building, and the platform was raised off the ground. It was right at the level of the train doors, so the people getting off didn't have to use boxes to get down.

Beyond the station, J. C. could see some of the town. It had tall brick buildings with signs over the doors. J. C. counted the rows of windows. Most of the buildings had two or three stories. Was this Cleveland? He turned back to his mother. "Mama, are we there?"

She smiled at him. "Not yet, baby. We have a long way to go."

J. C. watched the people get off and on. Everyone settled down, and the train moved again. J. C. tried to count the houses as they left the city, but the train got faster and faster. Whoosh! The world sped up past their windows. They left the city and went through forests. They had different kinds of trees than the woods back home. J. C. watched for a while, but it started to get dark outside. Mama was asleep, with her head against the wall.

J. C. remembered the cars in back, with the seats that turned into beds. He leaned over the bench in front of him and poked his brother Sylvester. "Psst! You want to go back and look at the other cars? The ones with beds, and the restaurant?"

Sylvester sat up. "Let's go!"

They went quietly through the next car, which was also full of black people. Many of them were asleep, leaning against one another or curled up on the bench.

The boys stopped between that car and the following one. J. C. couldn't read very well, but he knew what the sign above the door said: WHITE. Would they get in trouble for going in there?

The boys peered through the window. It looked like everyone was sleeping. "Come on," Sylvester said. "We'll just be real quiet."

They opened the door and slipped through. They tiptoed down the aisle past all the sleeping passengers. One woman opened her eyes and glanced at them, but she just gave a little smile. The boys made it through the car, and paused in the space before the next one.

Sylvester grinned at J. C. "Whew! I wonder how many more of these there are."

They crept into the next car. This time, they only got a few steps before someone called out, "Hey you boys! What do you think you're doing?"

They turned to see a young white man, wide awake. He'd been in the front corner, hidden from the window.

J. C. gave his friendliest grin. "We don't mean no harm. We just want to go to the dining car."

"That's no place for you," the man said. "This section is for white folks. You get back where you belong."

J. C. looked around. Other people were awake and watching. They didn't look friendly. J. C. was suddenly aware of his patched clothes. He kept smiling as he and Sylvester backed toward the door. They slipped through it and then tiptoed through the next "white" car. They didn't stop for breath until they were safely back in a "colored" car.

The boys looked at each other. "It's not fair," Sylvester said. "I wanted to see the beds on the train."

"Me too," J. C. said. "We weren't hurting nothing." It didn't seem fair that the boys couldn't even go look. J. C. wondered if the whole world was like that, divided into black and white. People said the North was better for black folks. But this train was going north, and it was just the same. "Maybe I don't want to be a porter after all," J. C. said. "I don't want to work for men like that one. I want to do something where people won't care what I look like, only what I can do."

Into the Big City

J. C. slept, and when he woke again, people were stirring. He looked out the window and saw houses crowded together. "Mama, where are we?"

"We're coming into Cleveland. Step lively now."

They gathered their bundles off the luggage rack, all ready to leave the train. But the train kept going. The houses got even closer together. Some buildings had four or five stories, just like Prentice said. The buildings seemed to go on forever. Did people really live and work in all of them? J. C. had never imagined putting that many people in one place.

In the distance, tall towers spewed smoke into the sky. The buildings got bigger. Many buildings were made of brick, but they looked dirty. They were almost black with smoke. J. C. pressed his face to the window so he could see everything. Some of the buildings looked as wide as the train was long. He tried to count the rows of windows. Six, seven, eight . . . he lost track.

"Mama, what are those places? Do people really live there, all the way up in the top?"

She peered past him. "I don't know, baby." She pulled him close and hugged him. J. C. tried to squirm away so he could look out the window more. But Mama wouldn't let go. J. C. realized she was trembling. He looked into her face, trying to read her mood. She couldn't be scared, not Mama. She must just be excited to finally reach that better place.

At last the train slowed to a stop. The train station was bustling with people, but J. C. didn't have time to watch. They gathered all their belongings and joined the throng leaving the train.

"Ida!" Mama called. "Don't you wander ahead. Sylvester, J. C., I want you right by my side. We got to stay together. I lose you here and I might never find you again."

They went along with the crowd, hardly knowing where they were going. They wound up in a huge room with the ceiling high above. Mama hustled them to a corner away from the crowd. They leaned against the wall and watched as the people rushed by. J. C. felt like his eyes were popping out of his head. There were more people in the train station than in all of Oakville. J. C. saw black people and white people, but other types too. He saw people unlike any he'd ever seen before.

And he never knew there were so many rich people in the world. Lots of men wore suits

and hats. Dozens of the women dressed like the landowner's wife back home. Some had animal fur draped over their shoulders and feathers in their hats. It wasn't just the white people who dressed up, though; there were plenty of black men and women with fancy clothes and shiny shoes walking through the station.

J. C. was glad that he was wearing his church clothes. He still felt embarrassed to have people see him. Everyone must know that he was a poor boy from the country.

But now they were in a better place, and that would change. Someday he would have a nice suit of his own.

J. C. wanted to run around and look at everything, but Mama held him close. He stared up at the high ceiling. Electric lights shone everywhere. A booming voice told people which trains were leaving from which tracks.

"What do we do now, Mama?" J. C. asked.

She didn't answer. J. C. looked at her. Mama wasn't a big woman, but somehow she seemed even smaller now. She pressed back against the wall and hunched over herself. Her eyes darted all around, and her mouth was turning down at the corners.

J. C. couldn't believe it. Mama looked scared.

"Mama?"

She looked down at him, her eyes huge. "I don't know. I don't know what we do. How can we find your daddy in all this crowd?"

J. C. stared at her. Then he looked around the room. He hadn't thought about that. They were going to Cleveland, to meet Daddy and Prentice and Quincy. It sounded easy. But how did you find anyone in a city this size? What if Daddy didn't get the letter about what train they were coming on? Would they have to stay in the train station for days and wait until Daddy found them? Would the train people send them back home?

The children huddled close to Mama, just watching and waiting. They couldn't think of anything else to do. J. C. didn't want to run around now, for fear he wouldn't find his way back. He didn't want to lose Mama, too.

Mama was praying in a soft voice. J. C. looked at Sylvester. What could they do to help?

Sylvester said, "Mama, I'm going to go to the top of those stairs and look."

"No!" Mama said. "You'll get lost."

"No, I won't," Sylvester said patiently. "I'll be able to see you the whole time. And you'll be able to see me."

"I'll go with him," J. C. said.

Mama looked at them. Finally she nodded. "All right. But only go where I can see you. And come right back!"

J. C. took Sylvester's hand, and they crossed the floor. People brushed past the boys without even looking at them. Some of the people smelled sweaty, and some smelled like flowers or spice. It was amazing how everybody moved so fast, all in different directions, but they never crashed.

They reached the stairs and went up. At the top, they stood next to the banister and looked out over the crowd. J. C. felt dizzy for a moment. It was like being at the top of a tall tree, only inside a building at the same time. He stood close to Sylvester. He looked out across the floor to where his mama and sisters stood. J. C. grinned and waved.

Sylvester and J. C. studied the people in the room. There were so many, and they were moving so fast. Still, J. C. knew he would recognize his father anywhere, even in a crowd. But he didn't see him.

"What if he doesn't come?" J. C. asked.

"He'll come," Sylvester said. "Of course he'll come."

"But what if something happened to him?"

"Then Prentice or Quincy would come. Don't you worry. They'll be here."

J. C. kept watching the crowd searching for his father and brothers. The voice kept booming out messages. "Chicago Special leaving from track six." J. C. wondered where the voice was coming from. It seemed to be everywhere. "Samuel Robinson, please meet your party at track nine."

J. C. tugged at his brother's sleeve. "What did that mean, 'please meet your party'?"

Sylvester's forehead furrowed. "I guess it means that man is supposed to go to track nine to meet someone."

They wanted to meet someone, J. C. thought. The messages echoed through the whole train station. If they sent a message, maybe Daddy would hear it.

"Sylvester, how do we send one of them messages?"

Sylvester shrugged. "I don't know, I never been here before either."

J. C. turned to watch the people coming up the steps. A black woman in a pretty dress glanced at him and smiled. She looked like she lived in the city and would know a lot. J. C. smiled at her. "Ma'am? Can you help us?"

She stopped. "What's the matter? Are you boys lost?"

"No, ma'am," J. C. said. "But we think maybe our daddy is lost. He was supposed to meet us here, and he's not here." He pointed across the room. "That's our mama over there. She's worried."

"I don't blame her," the woman said. "But how can I help?"

"How do we make one of them messages?" J. C. asked. "The ones everybody can hear."

"Now you are a smart boy," the woman said. "Your daddy will be real proud of you." She pointed over the railing. "See that office? You go up to them and say you want to page someone."

J. C. and Sylvester thanked her. J. C. waved to his mother, and the boys went down the stairs. A few minutes later, the message boomed out over the room. "Mr. Henry Owens, please meet your family in the main lobby."

J. C. and Sylvester ran back to their mother. "Did you hear that, Mama?" J. C. said. "Daddy will find us now."

Mama hugged him tight. "I sure hope so. I hope he's here and can hear it."

And then they heard a shout. Daddy, Prentice, and Quincy were running toward them. Soon they were all hugging one another and talking at once. Mama was crying.

When they finally calmed down, Prentice said, "It's a good thing you had us paged. We looked all along the train, but you must have gone past before we got there. We didn't know what to do next."

"It was J. C.'s idea," Sylvester said.

But J. C. already had something else on his mind. "Prentice! Where did you get those new shoes!"

A New Name for a New Life

They stepped outside, and J. C. wrinkled his nose. Cleveland smelled funny. Besides all the people smells, J. C. could smell garbage, like a pig's slop bucket. Underneath was the smell of smoke. Not nice smoke like from the stove back home, but heavy, dirty smoke. When he looked up, he could hardly see the sky between the big buildings, and the sky he could see looked gray. "Is there a fire?"

Prentice laughed. "That's just smoke from

all the factories. You'll get used to it. It's the smell of jobs."

They took a streetcar across town. J. C. stared at all the strange people. He tugged at Prentice's sleeve. "Look at that man," he whispered. "I never seen anyone like him."

Prentice leaned down and whispered back. "He's from China—on the other side of the world."

J. C. watched a couple of white men with black hair. It sounded like they were arguing, but J. C. couldn't understand a word.

"What are those people saying?" he asked Prentice.

Prentice glanced at the men. "That's Italian they're talking. They're from another country too, in Europe. You'll see lots of them where we live, and Polish families, too. People from other places as well, but mostly Italians and Poles."

Mama clutched her bag tighter. "It's like a foreign land!"

Finally they got off and walked the rest

of the way to their new home. The narrow streets were crowded with people walking. More people sat on steps visiting. Few of them sounded like the folks back home. Sometimes J. C. could understand the words, but the accent was different. Sometimes he had no idea what they were saying.

"I didn't know the North had so many people who aren't even American," he said.

"They are American now," Prentice said. "They came here to find work and a better life, just like us. The Urban League helped us find jobs."

"And J. C. and Sylvester will go to school," Mama said. "I've always wanted my children to go to high school."

"They'll need to work, too," Daddy said softly. "The steel mill don't pay that well, and things are expensive here."

"They can work evenings and weekends," Mama said. "They go to school first."

● ● ●

J. C.'s mother, who had always been so strong, was afraid of the big city. At first she would only leave the house to shop for food. Then she had to take one of her daughters with her. But they needed money, so after a few months, Mrs. Owens went to work as a maid. So did her daughters. They made twenty or thirty cents an hour.

The family didn't make much money, but they made enough. After a while, J. C. had new shoes and three shirts—not just one for work days and one for Sundays.

J. C. worked several part-time jobs in the evenings and on weekends. At a shoe repair shop he swept floors, washed windows, cleaned machinery, and shined shoes. He also pumped gas at a filling station. His favorite job was working at a greenhouse. It was a little bit like being back in the woods in Alabama. The greenhouse had some baby oak trees. Oakville had been named for all the oaks that grew there. It was funny seeing little oaks inside

a building, but J. C. liked them. He imagined owning a house someday, with a big oak tree growing out front, but he laughed at the thought. When would he ever be able to get his own oak tree, and a place to plant it?

J. C. started school. The elementary school was only three blocks from home. It was a large brick building, with different rooms for each grade. J. C.'s sister Ida brought him to school. The principal glanced at J. C. "Alabama, huh. We'll put you in the first grade."

"But he's nine years old!" Ida said.

"And he's been to school in rural Alabama," the principal said. "He'll start in first grade here."

Ida looked down at J. C. and shrugged. They went to the first-grade classroom. J. C. smiled shyly at the other students. Unlike his Oakland school, different races sat in the classroom together.

The teacher, a pretty young woman, showed him a seat. J. C. was small for his age, but he was still bigger than the other children. He could barely fit behind the tiny desk. The teacher asked his name.

"J. C., ma'am," he whispered in his Southern drawl.

"Did you say Jesse?" she asked.

"J. C., ma'am."

"Speak up a bit. Your name is Jesse, is that right?"

J. C. felt the other children staring at him. He didn't want to cause trouble, or make this nice woman angry. "Yes, ma'am, Jesse Owens." He would be known by that name from then on.

The teacher quickly found that Jesse could read and write a little. She moved him up to the second grade. He was still a couple of years older than his classmates. Even so, he struggled to catch up. He realized that he had not learned very much in Oakville, where school closed every time the fields needed work.

His Cleveland school focused on citizenship, discipline, and manners. Most students were immigrants from southern and eastern Europe. The school tried to Americanize them. Academics came second. But Jesse enjoyed school, and got along well with the other children. He quickly became best friends with a boy named Dave Albritton. Dave was also from Alabama, only a few miles away from Oakville. They both loved sports.

The school athletic coach was named Mr. Charles Riley. He was a thin white man, not very tall, with round glasses and gray hair. Sometimes Jesse saw Mr. Riley watching as he and Dave played on the playground.

When Jesse was in the fourth grade, Mr. Riley called him over. "I've been watching you," he said with an Irish accent. "How would you like to join the track team and build up those skinny legs of yours?"

Jesse grinned. "I sure would!" He didn't expect to be very good. He was getting stronger, but he was still one of the skinniest kids in school. But he didn't care. It would be a chance to do something for fun, outside of school and work.

He couldn't wait to tell his mother that evening. She listened, and then shook her head. "I don't like it, J. C." She was the only one who still called him that.

"Why not, Mama?"

"You might get hurt. You're not built like your father or brothers. You've been sick too often."

"But Mr. Riley said running would make me strong," Jesse said. His mother just shook her head.

That night, Jesse waited until his father was sitting alone out on the porch. He told him about Mr. Riley, and what Mama had said.

His father frowned. "I don't know, Jesse. Your mama's right pretty often."

"I know," Jesse said. "But I want to grow up to be strong. I want to be a good runner like you were."

His father looked at Jesse for a minute, then turned and went into the house. Jesse sighed. Running was fun, and it would be exciting to be part of a track team. But it didn't look like that would happen.

In the morning, Jesse's mother took him aside. She said, "I don't know what's got into your father, but he wants to let you do this running. You be careful, though."

Jesse ran all the way to school and found Mr. Riley. "I can run!" he said. "I can join the team."

"That's fine," Mr. Riley said. "You'll have to work hard every day, running and doing exercises. Report to the field after school."

Jesse's heart sank. "But Mr. Riley, I can't come after school today. I work at Wright's filling station this afternoon."

"I see," Mr. Riley said. "Well, tomorrow then."

"Tomorrow I work at the greenhouse. Two days I run errands and deliver groceries. And on Saturdays I have to—"

Mr. Riley interrupted with a laugh. "If you run as hard as you work, I'll have a champion on my hands. How about before school? If you get here forty-five minutes early, so will I."

Jesse agreed.

Four Years from Friday

At first Jesse coughed a lot when he ran. He tired quickly, even during short runs. He couldn't imagine why Mr. Riley would go to so much trouble for him. But Jesse didn't want to disappoint his coach and he still dreamed of being a good runner.

Slowly, as the months passed, Jesse's legs got stronger. His lungs got better too. He went a whole winter without getting pneumonia, that dreaded "devil's cold" that had almost killed him several times.

Mr. Riley's training was just as important

as Jesse's hard work. "Don't worry about running fast," Mr. Riley would say. "Just run right. Then the speed will come by itself. Run like you're on a red-hot stove. You don't want your feet to touch it, but they have to. So lift up those feet just as soon as they touch that stove."

"But will I ever be fast enough to compete?" Jesse asked. "And maybe even win?"

"Just keep training," Mr. Riley said.

"But I'm nowhere near as fast as the others," Jesse said. "I'll never make it this year."

"Who says we're trying to make it this year?" Mr. Riley said. "Don't just train for Friday's race. Train for four years from Friday." That's what he always said. "Four years from Friday" didn't mean any specific date. It just meant train for the future.

Jesse kept working hard, and he got better. He wondered how fast he was. After running the 100-yard dash, Jesse would sometimes ask, "What was my time?"

Mr. Riley always said, "Oh, about thirteen or fourteen seconds. I didn't get it exactly." The best runners ran the 100-yard dash in under eleven seconds.

Once, Jesse was sure he'd run especially fast. Mr. Riley was staring at his stopwatch as Jesse stumbled over. Jesse gasped, "Gee, my time must have been better than thirteen seconds on that one, Mr. Riley!"

Mr. Riley gave a small smile. "A little bit. You are improving, but we still have a long way to go. See you tomorrow."

On another day, Mr. Riley told Jesse to invite his parents to a school race. Jesse's father was working at a loading dock, but his mother did extra work the day before so she could be there. Jesse ran his best, to show her how strong he was getting. He finished the race several steps ahead of the next runner.

Mr. Riley took Mrs. Owens aside and told her softly, "Your son has the most unusual pair of twelve-year-old legs I've ever seen.

This may shock you, but Jesse could become a champion."

Mrs. Owens didn't say anything to Jesse. She didn't want to get his hopes up for a thing that sounded so impossible. Still, she gave him an extra-tight hug before she left.

By the time Jesse finished elementary school, he was one of the fastest runners in his class. He looked forward to racing at Fairmont Junior High School. The track team competed against different schools, and people paid attention to the races. The newspapers even printed the times. Then Jesse had proof that he was getting faster, but he wasn't winning races. He was competing against older boys, in longer races such as the quartermile. Jesse often got off to a fast start, pulling ahead of the others runners, but he couldn't keep his lead. After about one hundred yards he could hear the others coming up behind him. He tried even harder, but they pulled ahead, and he couldn't catch them again.

He didn't think too much about the future. Mr. Riley could talk about "four years from Friday," but Jesse mostly worried about today. In just a few years he would have to leave school and get a full-time job, like his brothers. Running in races was something to enjoy while he could, while he was still a kid. There couldn't be a future in it.

Then one day the school had a special visitor. A runner named Charley Paddock gave a speech to the students. Paddock had competed with the University of Southern California. In the early 1920s, Paddock had held every important sprint record. He won the gold medal in the 100-meter dash at the 1920 Olympics in Belgium. Four years later, he won the silver medal in Paris. The newspapers had called him "the world's fastest human."

A new world opened for Jesse as he listened. He imagined racing in college. He thought of traveling to other countries to compete. He dreamed of going to the Olympics, and maybe even bringing home one of those medals.

After the speech, Mr. Riley introduced Jesse to Charley Paddock. Jesse listened in awe as the two older men talked. Jesse and Paddock looked nothing alike. Paddock was white, with a thick, muscular chest. Jesse was young, black, and skinny. But when Paddock left, Jesse said, "I'd like to be like him."

Mr. Riley smiled. "You can be a champion like him someday, if you work hard enough. But you don't want to run the way he does. He flails his arms and pumps his knees high. And he leaps forward to break the tape at the end. He isn't smooth. You're already smoother than he is."

"But he wins, and I don't."

"Keep training," Coach Riley said. "Remember, four years from Friday. The next Olympics is just about four years away."

For the next meet, Jesse wanted to do his

best. This would be the time he won. He glared at his opponents. He wanted to make sure they knew he meant to win.

But in race after race, other runners passed him.

Finally Jesse asked Coach Riley for help. "Why do I always fall behind? What am I doing wrong?"

Mr. Riley smiled. "I'm glad you asked. I want you to meet me on Sunday. You don't work Sunday afternoons?"

"No, just in the mornings."

"Good. I'll pick you up at one o'clock. We're going to go see the best runners in the whole world."

Jesse could hardly wait. Who would they see? Was an Olympic gold medalist visiting Ohio? Jesse went to the library to see a newspaper. He read the sports section, but it didn't say anything about visiting champions.

On Sunday afternoon, Jesse got into Mr. Riley's car. He had rarely been in an automobile. It was wonderful to see the scenery flying by, just like back on that train, for mile after mile. They drove for a couple of hours. Mr. Riley didn't talk much, but then he never did.

Finally they pulled up at a big building with no roof. Jesse had no idea where they were. Mr. Riley paid the entrance fee, and they went inside.

Jesse looked around at the crowd of people. Bleachers stretched to the sides. Ahead, in a wide-open ring, horses thundered past. They were at a racetrack.

Jesse stared at Mr. Riley. "We're here to see horses? Not people?"

"Watch the horses run," Mr. Riley said. "No man in the world can come close to them."

They leaned against a railing and watched the races. Jesse had grown up with farm horses, not racehorses. These beautiful animals ran with a fluid grace. The winners were the most beautiful of all. Jesse watched them carefully, studying every movement.

Coach Riley made soft comments as the horses flew by. "Look at the muscles in his neck. See how easy they're resting while he gallops?"

Finally they headed for home. Back in the car, Mr. Riley asked, "Well? What did you see?"

Jesse bit his lip and wrinkled his forehead in thought. "They move like they're not even trying. They make it look easy. But you know they are trying."

"That's right," Mr. Riley said. "And what about their faces?"

Jesse thought for a moment and then shrugged. "I don't know. I didn't see anything on their faces."

Coach Riley smiled. "That's right. Horses don't try to stare each other down. That's for actors. With a horse, it looks easy. That's because the determination is all on the inside, where no one can see it."

Jesse thought about that lesson all the way

home. He had been worrying too much about the other runners. He had been putting his energy into his face instead of his legs. He had to forget about the other runners and put his own emotions aside. He would work on being like a racehorse—graceful, fluid, and calm.

Jesse put everything he had into training. He was strong enough now to get a job delivering groceries after school. The job paid twenty cents more per hour, and also gave Jesse extra exercise. He had a two-mile walk home after work. He would run one block as fast as he could, then walk a block, then run again. His legs got stronger and more muscular.

His jumping got better first. In 1928, he made 6 feet in the high jump and 22 feet, 11 ¾ inches in the broad jump. These were new world records for junior high athletes. Jesse could tell that Coach Riley was proud, but all he said was, "Keep training."

"What should I train for next?"

"Why, for four weeks from Friday, of course."

Charles Riley was like a second father to Jesse. He sometimes brought Jesse home for Sunday supper with his family. He also taught Jesse about more than just running. He said, "To win a race, you have to go to your limit, and then go past your limit. That's the place victory is always found, because it's victory over yourself. You have a special talent. But a time will come when you'll be asked for more than ability. Then you have to give it everything you have—more than you think you can. You have to make up the difference, in manhood."

Jesse worked hard in school, but he still couldn't read very well. His grades were never great, but he passed. He had a problem with stuttering, but that didn't keep him from talking. He was friends with everyone. The other students elected him student council leader—something rare for a black student in a mostly white school. The teachers made him a school monitor. Even better than these honors, Coach Riley named him captain of the track team. Jesse felt like he was really somebody.

Though Jesse was doing well, times were tough for his family. The Great Depression started in 1929, making work harder to find. The steel mill cut back on its working days, so Jesse's brothers worked only four days a week, then three, then two. They found whatever other jobs they could—moving boxes or hauling trash.

Jesse's father, who had grown blind in one eye, stepped in front of a taxi and broke his leg. He spent a long time out of work, and even when his leg healed he had a difficult time finding a job again. People liked strong, young men for physical jobs, and Henry Owens was almost fifty years old and worn out from working in the fields. He had never learned to read or write, so he didn't have many options. Sometimes he got work as a garbage man, the rest of the time he spent looking for jobs. He didn't make as much money as his wife or children. Jesse could see it wasn't easy on him, that for his father, Oakville had been a better place. But he had done the hardest thing: He had left so his children could have a better life.

Sylvester had to drop out of school to work. Jesse's mother took in laundry to help pay the rent and keep Jesse from having to drop out too. She was determined that at least one of her children would finish high school.

Jesse entered East Technical High School in the fall of 1930. The school was only a few blocks from Jesse's home. Classes weren't too hard. Jesse didn't need to read or study much. The school focused on job skills such as auto mechanics and welding.

The coach, Edgar Weil, was young and new to the job and his specialty was football. Coach Weil asked Charles Riley to help run the track team. Coach Riley gladly became an assistant so he could keep working with Jesse.

Jesse's best friend, Dave Albritton, also went to East Technical High School. Dave's specialty was the high jump, and Coach Riley thought he might someday be world class. The boys dreamed about going to the Olympics together someday.

One afternoon, Jesse stepped through the school doors to find rain pouring down in a torrent. He paused under the overhang. He didn't mind getting wet, but he didn't want to show up at his job with his clothes dripping. It would look bad, and he didn't want to walk around in cold, sticky clothes for the rest of the day either.

A girl came through the doors behind him. Jesse watched as she popped open her umbrella. She was pretty, with her hair curled tight against her head.

She saw him watching and smiled. She glanced at the rain and said shyly, "Do you want to share my umbrella?"

Jesse hardly trusted himself to speak. He nodded, smiled, and stepped forward to take the umbrella from her. He held it as they walked close together, sheltered from the rain.

Jesse tried to study the girl from the corner of his eye. She was maybe a couple of years younger than he was. Her clothes were simple, but clean and pretty.

She glanced at him and smiled. "My name is Ruth. Ruth Solomon."

"Oh," Jesse stammered. "I'm Jesse Owens. Pleased to meet you."

"Which way are you going?" Ruth asked.

"To the grocery store. To work. But you don't need to go down there. I'll walk you home."

Ruth nodded. "Then you can take the umbrella, and bring it back after your job."

She smiled, and Jesse felt as if the sun had just started shining. He would get to see this girl at least once more! He searched his brain, trying to think of something else to say to her. He had noticed her Southern accent. "Where are you from?" he asked.

"Georgia," she said softly. "We haven't been here long. It's nice, though."

"I came from Alabama," Jesse said. "Sometimes I miss it, but mostly it's better here. I'm on the track team."

Ruth turned her big brown eyes on him. "That's wonderful. Maybe I'll come see you run sometime."

Jesse grinned.

That evening, after he'd returned her umbrella, Jesse went home and sat on the porch. He stared at the rain and could feel himself smiling. Sylvester came out and punched him on the arm. "What's up with you? Are you sick? I've never seen you sit so still."

Jesse looked up at him. "I met this girl. . . ."

"Oh, ho!" Sylvester whooped. He danced around on the porch. "Jesse is in love, Jesse is in love!"

Some of Jesse's other brothers and sisters came out to see what was going on. They started teasing Jesse too. He didn't care—it was the truth. He did feel like he loved Ruth Solomon. Maybe someday he would marry her. But he didn't tell Sylvester that.

Soon, Jesse was walking Ruth home from school every day, before going to his job. Her family was as poor as his, but Ruth always dressed neatly and seemed to see the best in the world. Each time he saw her, Jesse fell a little more in love.

About a year after Jesse watched the horse race, he got ready for a big race of his own. His school was competing against other high schools throughout Cleveland. Coach Riley wanted Jesse to run the 220-yard dash. Jesse trained for weeks. He would give it everything he had. Even more than he *thought* he had.

The track was circular, and once around

it made 220 yards. Jesse got in line with the other runners. He spotted Ruth sitting in the stands and waved to her. Then he crouched, digging his feet into the ground for a solid start. He kept his gaze ahead, on where he was going, not on the boys beside him.

When the starter's gun went off, Jesse exploded forward. He quickly took the lead. Instead of staying just ahead of the other runners, he pushed himself harder. It was impossible to sprint for a full 220 yards, but Jesse ran as fast as he could. He could feel his lead growing.

He came to a curve before the last straightaway. This was where a runner would coast a bit, saving something for the long, tough last stretch. Instead, Jesse pushed as hard as he could. Somehow, he would find enough strength later, when he needed it. He drove his legs harder. He strained his lungs and heart.

He came to the last straightaway. He should

have been tired, but he felt like he was running faster than ever.

But somehow, the other runners were catching up. Jesse could hear their shoes hitting the ground behind him. He reached inside himself for more strength and ran even faster.

The four other runners drew almost even with him. Jesse pushed himself. He refused to give up.

All four runners pulled slightly ahead of him. He started to fall behind.

No! I have to catch up! Jesse screamed inside his mind.

He was at their heels. One had dropped a half step behind the others. Jesse pulled even with him, and then passed him.

He was pulling even with the next two.

They crossed the finish line. Jesse felt the tape against his chest, loose and flapping because it had already been broken. He hadn't won.

The race was over, but Jesse couldn't stop. He had tried so hard to pass the other boys that he just had to keep running. He ran with all the energy he had, straight ahead. He ran until he hit the brick schoolyard wall.

Jesse didn't feel any pain from his bruised elbow or aching legs. All the pain came from trying his hardest, and losing. He had given everything he had, and was still beaten.

Jesse wanted to get out of there and be alone, but Coach Riley ran up to him. Jesse waited to hear what he had done wrong. Mr. Riley reached out and shook his hand. "Congratulations, Jesse."

Jesse stared. He knew the coach wouldn't make fun of him, but he didn't understand.

"I know," Mr. Riley said. "You think you lost today. But you're wrong. You won today. Do you know who you beat? You didn't beat him just once, either. You beat him a hundred times on that track. Even when the race was over, you kept going. You beat him one more time. You could beat your opponent today, but that doesn't mean you'll beat him tomorrow. It doesn't mean you'll beat him next week, or next year."

Mr. Riley leaned closer and lowered his voice. Jesse had never heard him talk so much at once. "If you do beat him tomorrow, and next week, and next year, if you keep winning, you'll go to the Olympics someday. But no matter how fast you are, you won't get there unless you can win like you won today. You know who you beat, don't you?"

Jesse knew. He had given the race everything he had, at every step, all the way to the end. He had won his own battle. He had beaten himself. Suddenly, the dream that seemed impossible a few minutes ago seemed within reach. Jesse knew that someday he would go to the Olympics.

Successes and Failures

Mr. Riley's lessons and Jesse's hard work started to pay off. One day, Jesse finished the 100-yard dash feeling like he had wings. He turned back to ask how well he had done. Coach Riley was holding his watch to his ear to make sure it hadn't stopped. Mr. Riley stared at the watch again. Then he got down and measured the track distance, to make sure it was really one hundred yards. He frowned and measured it a second time.

Finally he went over to Jesse and put a hand on his shoulder. "My boy, you have just done what no other high school athlete has ever done. You have tied the world record."

Jesse laughed out loud. "Coach, you always told me I was coming in at thirteen seconds or so. Was that true?"

Mr. Riley grinned. "Maybe you were a little faster than that. But I didn't want you to get too proud."

"Is that why you always had me run long races? Ones I couldn't win?"

"I wanted you to build up your strength and stamina. It worked, didn't it?"

Now that Jesse was entering the shorter races, he started beating older high school boys. His best event was the 100-yard dash. Soon, he was winning every time. The only question was how far ahead of the others he would be. Jesse liked winning, but most of all he simply loved the feel of running. It was a little like flying.

Jesse was becoming famous, at least in Cleveland. Sprinters from other schools

talked about his style and ability. People came to watch him run. The Cleveland *Gazette* reported his wins. Jesse also did well in the broad jump and the high jump.

In 1932, Jesse got his first shot at the Olympics. Americans were excited, because the games would be in Los Angeles. African Americans were especially interested. It looked like, for the first time, the U.S. team would include many black athletes. Jesse wanted to be one of them.

Jesse attended the U.S. Olympic team trials at Northwestern University, in Evanston, Illinois. In Cleveland, in high school track meets, Jesse was the star. He usually won far ahead of the competition. The Olympic trials were different. The best athletes came from across the Midwest. Many were older, taller, and stronger than Jesse.

"Look at him," Jesse whispered to his friend Dave. "That's Ralph Metcalfe, from Marquette University. He's set a lot of sprinting records.

He got a silver and a bronze in Los Angeles." Could Jesse really beat someone like that? The college boy seemed so worldly.

As Jesse got ready for the first race, Coach Riley put a hand on his shoulder. "Just do your best. Run right, like I taught you."

Jesse nodded, though he hardly heard the words. He was thinking, *I have to beat him. I have to win this race.*

Jesse burst from the starting blocks. He ran hard, straining every muscle. He was neck and neck with Ralph Metcalfe. For a second or two, he was in the lead.

But Ralph broke the tape just a moment before Jesse.

Jesse's heart felt like it would burst, not from the strain of running, but from disappointment. Still, he offered his hand to Metcalfe. "I thought I had you," Jesse said, gasping for breath.

Metcalfe smiled. "Maybe that's what beat you."

102

Jesse didn't make sense of that remark until later. Metcalfe was saying what Coach Riley always said: The mind is just as important as the body. Jesse had run his hardest, but he'd forgotten to relax. He had tightened up and worried about beating the competition, rather than just running the best race. He competed in the broad jump, and in the 100-meter and 200-meter sprints. He lost all three events.

On the long trip home, Jesse could hardly bear the pain of disappointment. "I've let everyone down," he said. "I just knew I'd go to the Olympics, and I didn't even make the team. Maybe I'm not as good as I thought I was. Maybe I'll never be good enough."

Coach Riley just said, "Four years from next Friday, Jesse. There's another Olympics in four years."

Metcalfe was one of eighteen black athletes who made the final trials for the U.S. team. Four of them won places on the U.S. Olympic track team. At the Olympics, Metcalfe finished third in the 200-meter race and second in the 100-meter race. Another African American, Eddie Tolan, won the 100-meter. Jesse read about it in the newspapers. He was glad for Ralph Metcalfe, but envious as well.

"We should have been there," he told Dave.

"Next time," Dave said. "You know what Coach says."

The boys grinned at each other and said together, "Four years from Friday!"

After the Los Angeles games, some European athletes stopped in Cleveland on their way home. They held a track meet against some American Olympians and local athletes. Jesse competed. He was able to relax at home, without the pressure of the Olympics. He won the 100-meter and 200-meter sprints. He wasn't competing against the top Olympic sprinters in those races, but still, they were the best from their countries. For the broad jump, he finished second to the Olympic gold medalist. Maybe, Jesse thought, he had a chance after all. In four years.

Something even more important happened that summer. Jesse became a father. On August 8, Ruth gave birth to a baby girl whom they named Gloria. Jesse was eighteen, and Ruth only sixteen. They hadn't really planned to become parents so young, and had to make some difficult decisions. Ruth dropped out of school to work as a hairdresser and take care of the baby. She kept living with her parents, while Jesse lived with his. They wanted to be together, but they both felt that Jesse should finish high school and go to college, if he had the chance. Then he could provide a better future for all three of them, and any other children they might have.

Jesse enjoyed his final year of high school as president of the student council and captain of the track team; he was popular among the other students. Of the seventy-nine races he ran in high school, he won seventy-five. Crowds would come to see him run. After one indoor meet, the Cleveland *Gazette* wrote, "Wherever Owens went, Saturday night he commanded attention. When at the far end of the hall, competing in the high jump, he stole the spotlight from the races and when racing he was the recipient of cheer after cheer from the extraordinarily large crowd."

Jesse finished off the year at the National Interscholastic Championship Meet in Chicago. He won the broad jump, with a jump of 24 feet, 9 ⅝ inches. He tied the record in the 100-yard dash at 9.4 seconds, and set a new world record of 20.7 seconds for the 220-yard dash. East Tech won the meet with fifty-four points. Jesse earned thirty of those points.

The team returned to Cleveland tired but happy. Jesse celebrated with his family, then visited Ruth. They stayed up late talking. "Sometimes I can believe it," he told her. "I can believe I really could be a world champion. This could be what I was meant to do."

Ruth took his hands. "I believe it. I always did believe in you. Lots of people do. You're a hero to the school. To the city, even. This is what you were meant to do. Not just for yourself, but for all of us. You inspire people."

Jesse shook his head. "Who would have thought people would even know my name?"

The next morning, Sylvester burst into Jesse's room and shook him awake. "Jesse, come on! They're having a parade. For you!"

Jesse yawned and rubbed his eyes. "What are you talking about? What parade?"

Sylvester jumped on the bed and sat on top of Jesse. "Don't you hear me? The city is having a parade in your honor. The mayor is going to speak. They're sending cars for us all. Now get up!"

Jesse laughed. "All right, I will, if you'll get off of me."

Sylvester rolled off and headed for the door. "Hey, wait," Jesse called. "What do I wear for a parade? My church clothes?"

Sylvester grinned. "No, wear your tracksuit. Let all the girls see your handsome legs." He laughed and ducked out the door as Jesse threw a pillow at him.

Jesse hardly had time to wolf down some breakfast before a shiny black convertible with the top down arrived at the door. Jesse sat in the backseat, with his mother and father. Sylvester sat in front, next to the driver. His other brothers and sisters piled into a second car.

As they pulled out, Jesse said, "Wait a minute. We have to get Ruth." He gave directions to the driver, and they swung past Ruth's house. Jesse bounded out of the car and knocked on the door.

Ruth stepped out, her eyes wide with amazement. "Jesse, what's happening?"

"It's a parade, and you're coming with me."

She laughed as he pulled her toward the car.

Finally they met up with the rest of the track team, where the parade would start. Jesse's teammates shared two cars. Coach Riley was there, and Coach Weil. Jesse had the place of honor, in the front of the line. He sat up high on the back of the seat so everyone could see him. They drove slowly past crowds of cheering, waving people, toward city hall, where the mayor would give his speech.

They cheered for the team and they cheered Jesse's name. Ruth smiled up at him. "What were you saying last night, Jesse? Who knows your name now?"

College at Last

It looked like Jesse would reach his dream of going to college. The question was, which college? Everyone seemed to have an opinion.

One Sunday evening, the family sat on the porch after dinner. Many of Jesse's older brothers and sisters had married, but they still lived in the Owens household. Housing was expensive, so the boys brought their wives home.

Prentice shook the pages of a newspaper. "Did you read this?" he asked Jesse.

Jesse shook his head.

"They're talking about what college you should go to," Prentice said. "They don't want you to go to Ohio State." He read aloud from the *Chicago Defender*, a black newspaper. "'He will be an asset to any school, so why help advertise an institution that majors in prejudice? You must realize that in the age in which you're living, a militant spirit against prejudice in all its forms must be shown.'"

"Aw, come on," Jesse said. "I don't want to be a politician. I just want to win races."

"Can't you do that at a black school?" Sylvester asked.

"There isn't one with a good track program," Jesse said. "Coach Riley says most don't have enough money to pay for good coaches and tracks, and for travel to track meets. Most of them like football better, anyway. But even with football games, white people don't watch. The teams only play against other black schools."

"You're right," Prentice said, "you have to go

to a good school. You need to compete against the best runners in the country, black or white. But they say the whole city of Columbus is as bad as the South. I've heard awful things about Ohio State. Black students can't share campus housing with white students. They made a black football player sit out of a game just because the other team didn't want to play against blacks. And you know there's only a hundred black students there, out of about fourteen thousand."

Jesse shrugged. "I'm used to that. It's mostly white students at East Tech. Lots of them are my friends. Why should college be any different?"

"What does Riley say?" Prentice asked.

"He'd like me to go to the University of Michigan. But I'd rather stay in Ohio, close to all of you."

"Close to Ruth," Sylvester snickered.

Jesse grinned. "Her too, and little Gloria. Anyway, Dave is heading to Ohio State and is going to join the track team. We'll be all right. Ohio State is going to get me a job, and I'll be able to go this fall if I pass some tests. Otherwise I'd have to stay in high school for another semester."

Prentice sighed. "Well, I hope you'll be happy there."

Jesse spent the summer pumping gas, and then headed to college. He wasn't allowed to live in the dorms, so he shared a house with other black students. None of the restaurants near the university would serve blacks. Only one movie theater let them in. It was the worst theater in town, and they had to sit in the last six rows.

Jesse waited tables and worked in the library. He also got a job as an elevator operator in the State Office Building. Many of the college's athletes worked there because it was an easy job that paid well. But only white athletes could work in the front passenger elevator. Jesse worked the freight elevator in the back of the building.

Jesse saw the silver lining. He only had to move the elevator once an hour, to take the cleaning crew between floors. He spent the rest of his evening shift studying. Even so, with his poor education, college was hard for him. Classes were large, so he didn't get much help from the teachers, and he had a busy schedule, with school, work, and training.

The track coach also asked Jesse to give talks at local schools. With the help of a phonetics class, Jesse overcame his problem with stuttering. He quickly learned to speak well, with good grammar.

It was still hard at first for Jesse to stand up in front of people and talk about himself. He remembered the wonderful preacher from his youth and tried to speak with the same dignity and passion. He told stories about his life, making them better at each telling. One of his favorite stories was about the time his mother cut the bump off of his chest. The students stared at him wide-eyed while he described the pain and the bleeding. "That cutting turned out to be a good thing for me," he told them. "That bump might have crippled me, for one thing. But also, from that day on, no physical hurt or discomfort made much of an impression on me. In track practice, when my lungs burn and my legs seem like lead weights, I can still run one more lap or push a little harder."

He gazed out at the classroom, meeting the eyes of one student after another. "That's something you should remember. You don't know how much pain you can take, until you're tested. But pain isn't always bad, you know. When things are tough, just remember that it's life's way of preparing you for the future."

Over time, Jesse learned to enjoy his speeches. It was fun to see the impact he could have on young people, and the public speaking skills he gained would help him throughout his life.

When track season started in the spring, Jesse worked with Coach Larry Snyder. Snyder had been a star athlete in the 1920s. He might have made the 1924 Olympic team if he hadn't been injured. Snyder took up where Coach Riley had left off. He worked on Jesse's start, telling him to keep his feet closer together for a faster spring forward.

On the track, Jesse was a brilliant student. He listened closely, took suggestions without complaint, and worked hard. Jesse realized that if he was going to compete against the best athletes in the world, every movement had to be perfect. Before, he only listened for the starting gun, but Snyder taught him to watch the starter's eyes. When he squeezed them shut, Jesse knew the starter was about to fire the gun, and he would be ready to explode out of the blocks that instant.

Snyder was an expert at the broad jump. When they started training, Jesse said, "Mr. Snyder? In high school I made twenty-four-and-a-half feet on the broad jump more than once. People say it's pretty good, but I think I can do better. Do you think I could get over twenty-five feet someday?"

Coach Snyder nodded slowly. "Twenty-five feet is just the beginning for you. Right now, your left leg is a little stronger than your right leg. You need to build up that right leg if you want to make a perfect jump. Get that leg strong, and you could jump twenty-six feet."

Jesse could hardly believe it. Most people thought a twenty-six-foot broad jump was impossible. But Jesse followed Coach Snyder's advice and quickly got past twenty-five feet. Then his progress slowed. One week he got half an inch farther. The next week, he didn't improve at all. But over the course of a year, he moved closer to the magic mark of twenty-six feet.

Pain Means Nothing

In May of 1935, Jesse was getting ready for his first National Collegiate Track and Field Championships. He and Dave couldn't wait. "We get to compete against the best athletes in the country!" Jesse said.

"We've been training hard," Dave said. "We're ready."

Jesse grinned. "You bet we are!"

They walked out of the house. Some of the fellows were playing a game on the lawn. "How about some touch football?" one asked.

Jesse glanced at Dave. "What do you think? We don't want to risk getting hurt."

Dave shrugged. "It's just touch football."

"Yeah, you're right. Let's go!" They ran to join the others.

The casual game was a nice break from all the competition. Half an hour later, Jesse's side leaned together in the final huddle.

"All right, the game is tied," Dave said. "What should we do?"

One of the fellows nudged Jesse. "Let's give it to the sprinter here. Jesse can fake left and then go down the right sidelines. We'll all block for him."

They lined up. The ball went to Jesse. He darted left, then spun and headed right. He raced ahead of the players who reached out for him. Moments later, he sprinted across the goal line.

"Touchdown!" he yelled. His teammates cheered and ran over and jumped on him. Jesse staggered under their weight, laughing, until pain slashed through his back.

"Get off! Quick!"

Jesse doubled over. Dave grabbed his shoulders. "Jesse! Are you all right?"

Jesse gasped. "I'm—I'm not sure." He managed to straighten up. He took a few steps, but he could hardly walk from the pain.

"You'd better tell Coach," Dave said.

Jesse groaned but nodded. Dave helped him walk across to the campus. They found Larry Snyder and told him what had happened.

Snyder shook his head. "Rest up for a few days. Only time will tell whether you can compete on Saturday."

Jesse went home and collapsed on his bed. "It'll be all right," Dave said.

Jesse put his hands over his face. "I can ignore the pain if I have to. I've done that before. But what if I can't go to the meet? This was my big chance." He shook his head. "I can't believe I did something so stupid."

Dave patted his shoulder. "It's not over yet. You've got a week to get better. I'll get you a hot pad."

The days passed, and Jesse's pain persisted. Sometimes it moved down his leg or into his foot. He tried soaking in hot water, heat pads and rubdowns. By Saturday, he could walk upright, but his back hurt when he moved.

"What do you think?" Dave asked. "Can you run?"

"I don't know. It hurts pretty bad. I guess it'll be worse if I run." Jesse sighed. "But I'll go along, anyway. I can't just sit at home."

The team headed to Ann Arbor, Michigan. Jesse put on his tracksuit. Maybe, by some miracle, he would be able to compete. At least it was a warm day, so his muscles wouldn't stiffen.

He jogged around the track, grimacing against the soreness. Coach Snyder stopped him. "Jesse, you're hurt. I'm not going to run you today."

Jesse couldn't bear it. "Please, Coach, I have to run today. It's the national championships."

Snyder shook his head. "I know that better than anyone. And I know what you could do for the team—if you could run. But you can't. You could injure yourself so badly that you'll never race again. You know the Olympics are next year."

Jesse had thought a lot about the Olympics. But on that day, only the national meet seemed important. "Listen," he said, "just let me try the hundred. I can't hurt myself too much on such a short race. We can see how my back does."

Coach Snyder hesitated.

"I know I can do it," Jesse added.

"All right," Snyder said. "But if it hurts, you just ease up right then. Save it for other days."

Jesse lined up for the 100-yard dash with top athletes from around the country. He crouched and shoved his spiked shoes into the ground. Pain shot through his back, but he concentrated on the race ahead.

"Runners, take your marks," the starter said. "Get set."

Jesse lifted his body, his weight on his fingertips. From the corner of his eye, he watched the starter point his gun toward the sky. As the starter pulled the trigger, Jesse shot from his crouch. Before the echo of the gun died away, the runners were pounding down the track.

Jesse quickly took the lead. Each stride brought him farther ahead. He didn't even notice his back. It just felt good to be running again. The air rushed past him, and he felt like he was flying.

He sailed across the finish line in first place. People crowded around him. Jesse laughed out loud. To think he had almost stayed home! He should have remembered: No matter what was wrong, running made him feel better.

Coach Snyder grabbed him. "Jesse! You've tied the world record—nine and four-tenths seconds!" Two of the officials had actually timed him at 9.3 seconds. But the third had said 9.4, and only the highest number counted for a world record.

Jesse stared at Coach Snyder, too shocked to speak. Finally, he grinned. "I guess I need a backache more often."

Snyder laughed and pulled Jesse aside. "Do you want try the broad jump, too?"

"You bet! I've got a good feeling about this day."

"I don't want you hurt worse, though," Snyder said, "and I don't want to wear you out before the other events. Make just one jump."

Broad jumpers got three chances, and the best jump counted. If Jesse was going to jump just once, he would have to put everything into that jump. The world record for the broad jump was 26 feet, 2 inches. Jesse placed a handkerchief next to that mark. He'd never jumped that far before, but he wanted to come close. The handkerchief would show him how far he had to go.

He waited at the end of the runway leading to the broad jump pit. The wind was at his back, but a strong wind could disqualify the jump. He waited until the breeze died down.

He jogged forward, and picked up speed until he was going at a flat-out run. He shortened his last stride to hit the board perfectly. His body rose in the air, and he kicked his legs. He flew closer to the towel.

He flew over the handkerchief and landed past it. Jesse couldn't believe it. Could he really have matched the world record? Maybe he had put the handkerchief in the wrong place. Maybe the wind had moved it. He waited, hardly able to stand still, while the officials measured his jump.

Then they measured it a second time.

Finally the track announcer held up Jesse's

hand and said, "I wish to introduce a world champion." Jesse had broken the world record by more than half a foot, with a jump of 26 feet, 8 ¼ inches. The crowd came to its feet and roared with excitement.

People crowded around, full of questions. Only one question mattered to Jesse. Would he try for one more record?

He would. After a twenty-minute break, he lined up for the 220-yard dash. He wedged his spiked shoes against the ground. He waited for the starting gun to go off. When it did, he charged out of the start and took a quick lead. For the first part of the race, he was a stride ahead of the next two runners.

But his energy was failing, and his back was aching again. Halfway through the race, the next runner pulled closer to him.

Jesse reached inside and tried to find more energy. The other runner pulled closer. Jesse strained, again and again. He wasn't just trying to beat the other runner. He was trying to beat himself. He found every last bit of strength, and he used it all. Finally, he started to pull forward.

He was a yard ahead of the next runner when he broke the finish line tape. An official held up his stopwatch. "Twenty and three-tenths seconds!"

A second official looked at his watch. "Twenty point three," he agreed.

Jesse had broken the world record in the 220-yard dash by three-tenths of a second.

The crowd roared again. Dave whooped and hugged Jesse. Ralph Metcalfe shook his hand. "You did it, Jess. There are no more worlds left for you to conquer today."

Jesse grinned. He had matched one world record, and beaten two others. He felt on top of the world. But maybe, just maybe, it wasn't over yet. His lungs were burning, but he jogged over to Larry Snyder. "Coach, I know this might sound crazy, but I'd like to run the low hurdles, too."

Snyder looked at him. "You've done amazing things today, Jesse. But even your body can only do so much. In the hurdles, you have to jump as well as sprint. And you won't have much of a rest. There's only the two-mile run before the hurdles."

Jesse spoke softly. "I'll never have another day like this in my life, Larry." It was the first time he had ever called his coach by his first name.

Snyder smiled. "You're right. Get out there and have your day. But don't expect to tie any records. I'll be happy if you can win."

"So will I," Jesse said. But part of him wondered. The hurdles were not his specialty, and he hadn't trained as hard for them. But on that day, he felt like he could do anything.

Still, as he lined up next to the best college hurdlers in America, he began to doubt. Could he really beat them? What if he was too tired to even run well? A loss could hurt Ohio State, and ruin his perfect day. He could still back out. He could blame his back injury. No one would think less of him.

Charles Riley's words came back to him: "A time will come when you'll be asked for more than ability. Then you have to give it everything you have—more than you think you can. You have to make up the difference, in manhood."

The starter raised his gun in the air. Jesse rose onto his fingertips. Once again, he shot out in front. Once again, he gave it everything he had. Most hurdlers tried to skim the top of the hurdles, jumping just high enough to clear. Jesse's style was different. He flew high over the hurdles. That should have slowed him down, but his strong legs made up for it. He held the lead until his chest split the tape.

The previous record was 23 seconds. The officials announced Jesse's time: 22.6 seconds. Jesse had set his fourth world record of the day.

Dave and Ralph hugged Jesse and shouted his name. People cheered, no matter what team they had come to support. At the end of the meet, Charles Riley came down from the stands. The coach had come from Cleveland to see Jesse compete. He had tears in his eyes as he said, "My boy, you've made me very proud."

Respect

Jesse became famous that day. But days like that were rare. Over the summer, Jesse lost several races to one of his rivals. Eulace Peacock was another African American originally from Alabama. Peacock was taller and more muscular than Jesse. In the spring of 1935, Jesse and Eulace took turns winning the 60-yard dash and the broad jump. But that summer, Eulace beat Jesse five times in a row. Some people said that Eulace was the true champion, and that Jesse's power was already fading.

They met again at a race in Cleveland. The 60-yard dash was billed as a battle between America's two fastest men.

Jesse greeted Eulace and shook his hand. "I'm going to get you today. You wait and see!"

Eulace smiled. "We'll see all right."

They lined up at the start of the race. Jesse rose on his fingertips, all his energy ready to spring forward. He just had to win this race. He couldn't bear another loss. The starting gun went off, and he shot down the track. To his surprise, he couldn't hear or see Eulace next to him. He won the race easily.

Jesse stopped and turned. Other runners crossed the line behind him, but not Eulace. "What happened?" he asked an official.

"Peacock's starting blocks slipped. He dropped out of the race."

Jesse jogged toward Eulace, who walked to meet him. "Well, Jesse, I guess you won this one."

Jesse shook his head. "I don't want to win this way. We'll race again." He dragged Eulace to the officials and explained.

"But the race is over," the official said.

"People came to watch the two of us race," Jesse said. "We have to do it right."

The officials and the other runners talked. Finally they agreed. They would start the race over. The crowd cheered as they figured out what was going on.

Once again, Jesse took his place at the start. The gun sounded. Jesse and Eulace thundered down the track side by side. They broke the tape together. The judges ruled that Peacock had won by the smallest margin, in 5.5 seconds.

Again the crowds cheered. Eulace grinned and said, "Well, Jesse? Are you satisfied now?"

Jesse smiled back. "It's not our last race. I want to win, but I want to win because I did the best—not because someone else got unlucky."

"Well said," Coach Snyder said. "Your success means you have a responsibility. People are watching you. Not just on the track, but all the time. They'll be talking about you, so give them something good to talk about." The newspapers praised Jesse's sportsmanship. He didn't win the race, but he won respect. That felt pretty good too.

In the fall, Jesse went back to Ohio State and his jobs there. For the first time in his life, he had money of his own. He sent most home to Ruth and his parents, but he still had enough to buy an old 1914 Ford with his friend Dave. They grinned at each other when they bought the car for $32.50.

"Look at us," Dave said. "A couple of Alabama boys, with our very own automobile!"

But the car wasn't just for fun. When the team traveled for meets, they drove. The white athletes went in a couple of newer cars. The black athletes went in Dave and Jesse's car. Jesse loved races, but everything else about traveling was hard. Even in the North, blacks couldn't eat in most restaurants. They had to stay at the YMCA, while the white athletes went to a hotel. Black athletes could race against whites, but often couldn't use the locker room showers with them afterward. In the South, blacks weren't even allowed to compete against whites.

On one Friday in February, they had a meet in Indianapolis. They started driving before dawn. Dave looked ahead at the cars full of white students and shook his head. "We're good enough to compete with them and win races for our team. But we're not good enough to ride with them."

Jesse just shrugged. The white athletes were a nice bunch of fellows. They didn't even seem racist, most of the time. But they didn't bother to make sure the black athletes got fair treatment. People just accepted it, because it had always been that way.

The sun came out, warming the air. Jesse's mood brightened as well. They passed through little farm towns that were just waking up. *Like a giant flower*, Jesse thought. *Maybe today Indiana will open up for us too.*

Coach Snyder pulled the first car up to a restaurant. The other cars pulled in behind. Jesse and his black teammates sat back. They watched the white athletes get out, stretch, and head into the restaurant. They could see Coach Snyder talking to the woman behind the counter inside. He leaned toward her. She shook her head.

Coach Snyder walked slowly out of the restaurant. He looked toward Jesse's car and shook his head.

One of the athletes rolled down the window and called out, "What did they say this time?"

Snyder took a few steps forward. "She says the owner is out, and she couldn't take the responsibility."

The black athletes grumbled, but nobody was surprised. They hardly ever got to eat with the white fellows. They talked track and tried to ignore their stomachs. Ten minutes later, two of their white teammates came out. They had a stack of fresh bread and plates of fried eggs. They passed them through the window. "Now this is more like it," Dave said as they dug in.

Jesse was just bringing the first bite of egg to his mouth when he heard a bellow outside his window. "So this is why they wanted those extra orders!" Jesse looked up at a big man with an apron hanging over his fat belly. "They said it was for themselves, to eat on the road."

"You were paid, weren't you, Mister?" Dave asked.

"I don't want money to feed *you*!" he yelled. He reached in the car and grabbed the plates of food. Eggs and bread tumbled onto their clothes and the car seats and floor.

Dave wouldn't let go of his plate. The man pounded at it with his fist. Food flew everywhere.

Dave dropped the plate on the floor and leaped from the car. Jesse dashed after him and grabbed Dave just before he reached the man. Jesse held Dave's arms and whispered, "No, Dave, no."

Dave strained against him, then slumped back and looked at Jesse. "All right. What's one more time?"

The restaurant owner sneered and walked back to the restaurant.

Dave swiped angry tears from his eyes as he got back in the car. "Now we can eat off the floor. That's how it's supposed to be, right?"

Jesse hesitated. He understood how Dave felt. Sometimes he wanted to get out and fight as well. But a black man would go to jail for hitting a white man, no matter who had started it. Besides, Jesse couldn't forget how he was raised. His father had taught him to always be polite. His mother had taught him to be true to himself, no matter what happened. Church had taught him to turn the other cheek. Charles Riley had taught him to control his anger, and focus on the end of the race. Coach Snyder had warned him that the country was watching him. His actions brought shame or honor not only to himself, but to Ohio State and to all African Americans.

Jesse swallowed. "Coach will stop someplace else and get us something."

"That's not the point!" Dave shouted. "Can't we ever fight back? Are we always going to have to call them 'Mister'?"

"We are fighting," Jesse said softly. "We're fighting a bigger battle than this one little place. And we're winning, too. We're winning when we study and get our degrees. We're winning when we come in first in a race. We're winning when we show them what we can do."

Dave just grunted. But when they got to the

track meet, all the black athletes raced their hearts out. They ran for themselves, and they ran to prove something to the world. Jesse won all his events. Even better, he felt the joy that running always gave him.

Lots of people came up and asked for his autograph. One white man handed Jesse a Bible. "Would you put your name here, Mr. Owens?"

Jesse stared at the man. Did he have a restaurant that wouldn't serve blacks? Or a store that wouldn't sell to blacks? Did he work for a company that only let African Americans in the back door, for deliveries? Did he live in a neighborhood that didn't sell houses to anyone with dark skin?

Jesse smiled at the man, signed his Bible, and shook his hand. Maybe that man felt a little different than he had the day before. Maybe it was one more win in the big battle. After all, he had called Jesse "Mister."

Racism Everywhere

America wasn't the only country suffering from racism. Across the ocean, something was happening that threatened Jesse's Olympic dream. Back in 1932, the International Olympic Committee agreed to hold the 1936 Games in Germany. In 1933, Germany's Nazi party had taken power, under Adolf Hitler. Hitler thought that northern European whites were better than other races. He said the ideal people were tall, blond, blue-eyed "Aryans."

"Have you been keeping up with the situation in Germany?" Dave asked Jesse one day.

Jesse shrugged. He didn't have much inter-
est in politics. "I've heard that Hitler is up to
some nasty stuff, but no one seems to know
what's really going on. It's probably just a lot
of talk."

Dave spread out a newspaper. "This says
they've been taking rights away from Jewish
people. Some people think that Hitler wants
to wipe out all the Jews."

"Naw." Jesse looked over Dave's shoulder.
"No way he could do that, could he? And why
would he want to, anyway?"

"I don't know, but there's more. The
Germans don't want to compete against black
athletes. They're saying that we should be
kept out of the Olympics."

"They wouldn't do that!"

"The International Olympic Committee is
threatening to take the Olympics somewhere
else if Hitler doesn't change his tune. I wonder if
they really would, with the Olympics so close."

Jesse shook his head. "Gee, Dave, when did

we get caught up in this kind of thing? I just want to run."

David grinned at him. "We've always been caught up in race issues. You just have that amazing ability to forget about the bad things that happen to you."

Jesse smiled back. "I guess so. But what good does it do to hold a grudge? I'd rather think about tomorrow than yesterday."

"Well, you better keep a close eye on tomorrow. We might not get to the Olympics at all, if Hitler has his way."

Every day Dave got a newspaper and read aloud the updates on the Olympics. Finally, Hitler agreed that all people would be welcome. "But listen to this fellow," Dave said. "He says the games will prove his theories. His team of Aryan athletes will show that they're better than everyone else."

"Do you think they could do it?" Jesse asked. "I haven't heard of a lot of great German athletes."

"He's keeping them secret. At least, that's the rumor." Dave ran a hand over his head. "And there's more. Some people are still saying that America shouldn't go. They say we should boycott the Olympics. That would send a message to Hitler that Americans don't agree with his ideas."

Jesse sat up on his bed. "Who wants the boycott?"

Dave glanced down at the paper. "The Amateur Athletic Union says we should boycott. The International Olympic Committee and the American Olympic Committee don't want to boycott. They say politics should stay out of sports."

"Well, I think it should too. But if things are as bad as they say . . . I just don't know."

David looked up at his friend. "And no matter what happens, you'll be in the middle of it. You're one of America's stars right now. If you get behind the boycott, that side will think it's won. If you go, other athletes will

think it's all right to go. Especially the white athletes. If black athletes are willing to compete in Germany, why shouldn't *they*?"

Jesse leaned forward and put his head in his hands. "I've been training for this Olympics for years. I want to go more than anything. But I want to do what's right."

Dave stood up and paced the room. "I wish there were a clear answer. Even our black newspapers can't agree. A lot of black Americans could make it to the Olympics. Some say we should go and prove ourselves that way. Others say we should stay home in protest."

Jesse looked up. "Let's go see what Coach thinks."

They found Larry Snyder over at the track and discussed the problem. Snyder put an arm around each of them. "I understand that you want to make a point in Germany. But look, America is racist too. Sometimes you fellows can't compete in important meets here. Why should you give up your best chance of success, to protest Germany, when things aren't much better at home?"

"That's a good point, Coach," Jesse said. "But maybe I should be doing more to make a difference."

"Today you are sitting on top of the world. But if you boycott the Olympics, you'll be a forgotten man." Snyder looked deep into his eyes. "Go to Germany. Win. Come home famous, and then you can make a difference."

Jesse finally decided that if he made it in the finals, he would go. By competing in Germany, he could show the world that black athletes could be just as good as white ones.

At the Olympic trial finals, Jesse won all three of his events: the 100-meter and 200-meter dashes, and the broad jump. His old rival, Eulace Peacock, didn't put up much of a fight. Peacock had gained ten pounds after an injury. Then he had torn his hamstring muscle during a meet. At the Olympic trials, he had his leg tightly taped. He ran courageously, but he just couldn't perform.

"It's tough watching him," Jesse said. "He's trying so hard. He could have been the best."

Larry Snyder patted Jesse on the back. "It's hard to see a great athlete fail. But it's partly his own fault. He didn't take care of himself. You're careful with your training, and that's why you don't get many injuries. Now just keep it up until we get to the Olympics."

Dave Albritton qualified to compete in the high jump. Jesse's old rival and friend Ralph Metcalfe also made the team. They were among the nineteen African Americans to make the 1936 U.S. Olympic team. Ten of those were on the men's track team. Two more were on the women's track team. The others were boxers or weightlifters. They would take on Hitler's Aryan athletes and see who came out on top. Many Americans looked forward to the battle. Jesse got pushed out in front.

Newspapers around the world asked Hitler, "Who have you got to beat Jesse Owens?"

Finally, Hitler answered. Dave found Jesse to share the news. "He's done it, Jess! Hitler gave a name."

Jesse looked up from his books. "You mean the man who's supposed to beat me?"

"Lutz Long. He's a broad jumper. The rumors say Hitler has lots of top athletes that he's keeping secret. But he named Lutz Long as the man who would beat you."

Jesse thought about that, and finally nodded. "We'll see. But I sure would like to take home one or two of those gold medals."

A Hero to All

On July 15, 1936, Jesse boarded the luxury ship SS *Manhattan* with eight hundred other passengers. Jesse was leaving America for the first time in his life. He would miss Ruth, whom he had married the previous summer, and their baby. He knew that Ruth, his parents, and all his siblings would be reading the newspapers to find out how he did, but he wouldn't even get to speak to them for weeks.

Jesse stood at the rail as the ship left New York. The land got smaller, and then vanished. Jesse looked in every direction, and saw only ocean. He would not see America again until his fate had been decided at the Olympics.

Jesse turned away from the ship's rail. He thought about how far he had come, and how hard he had worked to get there. So many things had changed. He owned only one suit, but it was a flashy pinstripe. His many stylish pants and shirts would earn him a joking vote of "best dressed" from his Olympic shipmates. Jesse only had eight dollars in his pocket, but the poor boy from Alabama would never wear rags again. People he had never met knew about him. He had found something he loved doing. It didn't matter if he was black or poor. He was somebody.

The trip lasted more than a week. The athletes didn't have much to do. Some ate rich food and drank champagne. They gained a few pounds and got out of shape. One woman swimmer got kicked off the team for drinking.

Jesse wasn't interested in these indulgences.

He was seasick at first, and then came down with a cold. When he wasn't too sick, he exercised on the ship's deck to keep in shape. He was quiet and polite, knowing that the reporters on board would record his every move.

He missed his parents, wife, and daughter. He also felt nervous about the Olympics. The world was watching him. People expected him to win, and maybe even set new records. What if he failed?

Jesse tried to hide his fear and loneliness. He didn't want to discourage his teammates. He was glad for his friends Dave Albritton and Ralph Metcalfe. Coach Larry Snyder was there too. He wasn't an official Olympic coach, so he paid his own way. He wanted to be there to help Jesse—and see him win.

As a veteran of the 1932 Olympics, Metcalfe helped calm the younger athletes. "Those reporters will try to get you to talk about Hitler," Metcalfe warned. "Don't take the bait. We're here to win gold medals for our country, for our schools, and for ourselves. Focus on that."

Metcalfe's words echoed what Coach Riley and Coach Snyder had taught Jesse. Put emotion aside, and focus on the race. But now it was harder than ever. Jesse was competing in the top sporting event in the world. People expected a lot from him. And competing in Nazi Germany just made it worse.

After the ship docked on July 24, the athletes took an express train to Berlin. Jesse could hardly believe his eyes. The city had prepared well for the Olympics. It wanted to show the world how powerful Germany was. Banners with the Nazi swastika hung alongside the Olympic banners. Armed soldiers marched in the streets, keeping the crowds under control. Germany looked like a country ready for war.

The athletes took a tour of the nine sports arenas that would host the events. The largest, an enormous new stadium, could seat

110,000 people. Loudspeakers would blare news of the games for people who couldn't get tickets to watch.

Their bus pulled into the stadium. Larry Snyder put a hand on Jesse's arm. "Jesse," he said, "you might not get the welcome you're used to here. Remember, the Germans have been saying bad things about the American team."

"You mean they've been saying bad things about me, because of the color of my skin."

"That too. You can't let it bother you. These are Germans, and they're going to support Germany. You can't expect them to like you. Don't let anything you hear from the stands upset you. Just ignore them and focus on your events."

Jesse nodded. He tried so hard to be likable; it hurt when people hated him for no good reason. But he had faced racism before. He could handle it here. He had to.

They arrived and stepped out on the track.

Jesse tried to block out the whispers starting in the stands nearby. But then the chattering grew louder, and the crowd broke out into a chant, "Yesseh Ohvens! Yesseh Ohvens!"

It took him a minute to understand the German accent. Then Jesse turned and stared. Was it possible? They were cheering for him! He smiled and waved. It was nice to know that he was famous even here. It was nicer to know that not all Germans hated him just because of his skin.

Jesse kept smiling as they finished the tour. The Germans had new ways to time the events. A high-speed camera helped judge the track and swimming races. An electric board showed the times. The Olympics, which was started in ancient Greece, was now a modern event.

The American athletes spent a week training and getting used to being in Germany before the games began. They stayed in the Olympic Village, in a town a half-hour drive from the stadium, along with six thousand athletes from fifty-two other countries.

Women stayed in a large dorm, while the men lived in cottages of twenty-four people. Each cottage had a guide who spoke the team's language. Jesse and Dave roomed together. The rooms were comfortable and the food excellent. At the American cottages they got American food. Jesse ate plenty of bacon and eggs, ham, steak, fruit, and juice.

For the first time, Jesse saw a television set, which broadcast the games. Television was a new thing, and the quality was poor. The athletes looked like they were floating in milk. The newsreels were better. Every night, the Olympic Village movie theater showed the athletes their wins and losses before the night's film. They could also go see music acts and fireworks, read in the library, and exercise in the swimming pool or on the practice fields. They could visit doctors, dentists, or barbers. They could get massages. Buses would take them to the right stadium for their events. The Olympic Village had everything an athlete might want or need.

Jesse and Dave wandered around, checking out all the things they could do.

"Did you ever dream such a place existed in the whole world?" Jesse asked.

"Never." Dave thought for a minute. "But then it doesn't really exist. Not anyplace but here in the Olympic Village. People from every country, of every race, can get together as equals. We can eat together, work out together, even watch a movie together. But it's not like that in the rest of Germany. We wouldn't even be here, if Hitler had his way."

Jesse nodded. "I'm still glad we came, if only to see this. If it's possible here, maybe someday it will be possible everywhere. Do you think so?"

"We can hope so, anyway."

Jesse had never even imagined such a world. Now he was a part of it. One of the most famous parts too. He woke up to find people shoving autograph books through his open bedroom window. Jesse signed them politely until Coach Snyder came in and shooed them away.

Dave picked up a note that had been slipped under the door. He read it and laughed. "Hey, Coach, look at this. It's a marriage proposal for Jesse!"

Snyder shook his head and smiled at Jesse. "I can see you're popular here, despite everything. But don't start believing all the praise. You're too likable to let yourself be spoiled by the attention."

"But, Coach," Jesse said, "what am I supposed to do? I can't just turn them away."

"I can. Now, get dressed if you want to eat before we head to the stadium."

They took the bus to the stadium for the first of Jesse's races. For each event, he had to compete several times. For the 100-meter dash, the runners were divided into twelve groups. Each group raced, and the best runners went on to the semifinals. Then the winners of the semifinals would go on to the final race.

Snyder scanned the schedule. "You don't have to run until the twelfth heat, the last one."

"Great!" Jesse said. "I'll get to watch everyone else." For each race, he stayed on the sidelines and practiced his start as the gun went off. Then he watched the races, studying the style of the top runners. He liked knowing his competition. One of the best was Germany's Erich Borchmeyer. He looked more like a football player or bodybuilder than a sprinter. He won his heat in 10.7 seconds, and the German crowd cheered wildly. An American, Frank Wykoff, won another heat in 10.6 seconds. Wykoff had been the first man to run the 100-yard dash in 9.4 seconds. Jesse had tied his world record the year before. The 100-meter dash was slightly longer. The best time in any of the qualifying heats was 10.5

seconds, from a Dutch man. Jesse wanted to beat that time in his qualifying round.

At last, shortly before noon, Jesse stepped out onto the track. He used a trowel to dig small starting holes for his feet. The track was muddy from the drizzling rain. It wasn't the best surface for running or breaking records.

Again the Germans chanted, "Yesseh Ohvens!" as he took his place. But when the starter raised his gun, the crowd fell silent. The runners settled into their starting stances. The gun went off, and they sprang forward.

Seconds later, it was all over. Jesse knew he had won, and only waited to hear his time. It was 10.3 seconds, equal to the Olympic record. In the quarterfinals race that afternoon, Jesse did even better, winning in 10.2 seconds. The crowd roared and Jesse waved. People started murmuring about a new world record, but the officials disagreed. The runners had a wind at their backs, so the record wouldn't count.

Reporters rushed up to Jesse. "How do you

feel about the ruling? Didn't the Germans rob you of a new record?"

Jesse just smiled. He knew they were trying to get him to say something bad about the Germans. All he would say was, "It was a fair race. I'm happy with my time."

"Hey, Jesse," one of the reporters said, "come over here and get a picture with Helen. She just got cheated out of a new world record too!"

American Helen Stephens had finished her 100-meter trial race about ten meters ahead of her competition. Her time of 11.4 seconds would have set a new world record for women. Once again, the officials said that wind had aided the run, so the time wouldn't count.

Jesse knew Helen slightly from the boat trip. He shook her hand, and they posed for photographs together. "Perfect," the reporter said. "I can see the headline—'The World's Fastest Man and Woman.'"

After lunch, Hitler arrived at the stadium. The crowd roared as loudly as they had for Jesse's win. Jesse looked up at the short man with dark hair and a tiny mustache. He didn't look anything like the Aryan supermen he bragged about. Still, Jesse felt a chill as he watched this powerful man raise an arm to the crowd. It was strange to think that Hitler hated him, when they had never even met.

Minutes later, a German athlete won first place in the shot put. Hitler cheered and danced like a regular fan. He invited the athlete up to his private box and shook his hand. Later, he met two German women and some Finnish athletes who won medals.

But as the afternoon drew on, it looked like an African American would win the high jump. In the end, Jesse's friend Dave Albritton took the silver medal. Black athletes took the gold and bronze medals as well. Hitler quickly left the stadium before America's national anthem could be played.

American papers roared their outrage at this snub of their athletes. Hitler had to promise the International Olympic Committee that he would not meet with any athletes, not even German winners.

Jesse was too happy about his friend's win to worry about Hitler's slight. He and Dave celebrated that night. Jesse admired the silver medal. "Not bad. Now we'll just see if I can get something to wear around my neck!"

Jesse returned to the stadium on the second day of competition. He had to run the 100-meter dash two more times. He easily won his semifinal race. Then he bundled up in a sweat suit and heavy blanket to stay warm. At five o'clock, he would race against five of the fastest men in the world. His friend Ralph Metcalfe was one of them.

Rain fell, making the tracks soggy. Jesse's lunch was soggy too. With all their preparation, the Germans had forgotten one thing.

Athletes didn't have a place to eat in the stadium. They had to go back to the Olympic Village for lunch. But Jesse was in three events, each with several trials. He rarely had time to return to the Olympic Village. Instead, he and Larry Snyder brought along cold sandwiches.

Snyder frowned at his own limp steak sandwich. "Sorry about the food, Jesse. It's not what I would feed an athlete before a big race."

Jesse swallowed some milk and shrugged. "At least I'm eating, Coach. I've put up with worse."

Snyder smiled. "Yes, you have. Jesse, I've never met a man with such a cheerful attitude about life. How do you do it?"

Jesse thought for a moment. "Well, my mama always said that if you look hard enough for the devil, the devil will find you." He grinned. "I guess I try to ignore the devil so he can't find me!"

Snyder laughed. They finished their lunch, and Jesse did some stretching exercises. Finally he lined up for the race. He glanced at his competitors as they dug their starting holes. Every one of them wanted to take home a gold medal, but only one would win. Jesse gazed down the muddy track. He had worked eight years for this. Eight years, and it would be over in ten seconds. One mistake could ruin those eight years. Or this could be a dream come true.

The crowd screamed out Jesse's name. They yelled for the German runner, Borchmeyer, too. They grew quiet when the men laid down their trowels and got in line. At the sound of the gun, the runners flew forward. Jesse drew ahead by the halfway point. In a few heartbeats, it was over. Jesse won by a meter. Ralph Metcalfe took the silver medal, and Borchmeyer had to settle for the bronze.

The officials announced his time: 10.3 seconds, tying the world and Olympic records.

Jesse and Ralph hugged each other. In the stands, over 100,000 people stood and cheered "Yesseh Ohvens! Yesseh Ohvens!" as Jesse jogged around the track in a victory lap.

Jesse and Ralph walked together to the victory stand. Jesse took the highest platform. He bent while they put a medal around his neck and placed a laurel wreath on his head. Then someone handed him a tiny oak tree as a symbol of the growth of the Olympic games. Jesse remembered working in the greenhouse and wishing that he might have an oak someday. He had never imagined getting it like this.

Jesse straightened and stood calmly while "The Star Spangled Banner" played and the American flag slowly rose. At least he was calm on the outside. Inside, he was fighting back tears of joy.

The Longest Jump

The next day, Jesse ran two trial races for the 200-meter dash. The track was dry, and Jesse won both in 21.1 seconds, a new world record for a curved track. The other competitors went back to the Olympic Village to rest. Jesse stayed at the track to be ready for the broad jump trials that afternoon.

He tried to watch the other events and think about what he would need to do to win that afternoon. But something kept interfering— a name: Lutz Long. Hitler's great athlete, a superman groomed his whole life for this one event. Groomed to beat Jesse Owens and prove that Hitler's Aryans were better than blacks.

Jesse knew he should forget about Long and all the other athletes. He should concentrate on his own jumps and nothing else. But he found it impossible.

An American reporter ran up to Jesse. "Is it true about Hitler?"

Jesse frowned. "Is what true?"

"That the Olympic Committee asked Hitler to invite you into his box, and he refused. He won't shake hands with you."

Jesse glanced up at the dictator's box. It looked empty. "I don't know."

"All right, I won't quote you, but that's what I heard." The reporter ran off.

Jesse felt anger boiling inside of him. He wanted to show Hitler, and the world, what a black man could do. He wanted to destroy Hitler's superman, Lutz Long, in the competition. Jesse struggled to get control of himself. He tried to remember Charles Riley's advice: An athlete could use anger, but it had to be an icy cold anger. Jesse didn't feel cold. His anger felt like fire.

The athletes gathered near the broad jump pit. Jesse searched for Long. He scanned the other athletes and then stopped cold on a man wearing the German uniform. This was Hitler's ideal of Aryan "perfection." He was a couple of inches taller than Jesse, with blue eyes and sandy hair. His body was beautifully proportioned, and had the lean, toned muscles of a top athlete. This had to be Lutz Long. For a moment, Jesse just stared.

Long walked to the broad jump pit and took a practice leap. He exploded off the board with a graceful power. Jesse remembered the racehorses Charles Riley had taken him to see years before.

Long landed, laughing. Another athlete came up to Jesse. "You're lucky this is just practice. If they were measuring, he might have a new world record."

Jesse had to agree. That perfect body held a competitive spirit to match.

Jesse reminded himself that he was a top athlete too. He still held the world record of 26 feet, 3 ¼ inches. He would show that German what he could do.

Each athlete had three tries to jump at least 23 feet, 5 inches. If they made it, they would go on to the finals. Jesse had been jumping at least a foot farther than that at every practice and meet for the last two years.

Jesse loosened up for his first jump by jogging down the runway in his sweat suit. He just wanted to get a feel for the runway and measure his steps. He stopped when he reached the pit.

An official raised a red flag. Jesse's jaw dropped. They were counting that as a trial jump! Apparently the Olympics did not allow practice runs.

Forget it, he told himself. *You've fouled before. You have two more jumps.*

When Jesse's next turn came, he raced down the track and exploded into the air. He would show Long what he could do. He landed at least a foot past the qualifying mark.

Before he could rejoice, the official raised a red flag. "Foul!" Jesse had stepped over the edge of the takeoff board. His jump wouldn't count.

Jesse berated himself. He had been trying to prove something. He had been showing off, and it made him careless. Now he only had one jump left.

His stomach felt empty and sick. His legs felt like water. What if he didn't even qualify? Hitler would say he was right about Aryan supremacy. And somehow Jesse felt that if he failed here, it would ruin the rest of his Olympics. He would be too upset to do well in the 200-meter dash finals ahead. If he failed there, as well, would America forget about his gold medal in the 100? Would African Americans feel he had let them down?

Jesse glanced at Lutz Long, who was relaxed and laughing. He had qualified with his first jump, so he didn't need to make any more. Maybe he really was a superman.

Jesse wanted to be back home in Cleveland. That was where he belonged. This was where Lutz Long belonged.

Jesse put on his sweatshirt and walked away from the other athletes. He needed time to calm down and get his thoughts in order. His legs were shaking, and he clenched his jaw to keep his teeth from chattering. What was he supposed to do? If he jumped his hardest, he might foul again. If he played it safe, he might not go far enough to qualify.

The sounds of the stadium buzzed in his ears. Then Jesse heard his name called in a German accent. It was his turn, they were calling him to jump, but he wasn't ready. He closed his eyes and took a deep breath. He felt a hand on his shoulder.

Jesse turned to see Lutz Long. He was the

one who had called Jesse's name. Jesse stared into the eyes of his enemy. Lutz Long smiled. "What has taken your goat, Jazze Owenz?"

Jesse almost laughed, but he couldn't find his voice. Anyway, how could he tell this man, of all men, what was wrong?

"I Lutz Long," Long introduced himself. "I think I know what wrong with you. You are one hundred percent when you jump. Like me. You afraid to foul again. But do not worry. You do not have to be best in trials. You only need qualify."

Jesse heard his name called again. This time it really was the loudspeaker, calling him for his last jump. Jesse's panic threatened to boil over. "Yes, but how do I make sure?"

"Same thing happen to me last year. You draw start line whole foot back of takeoff board. Jump from there. Jump as hard as you can, but no way you can foul. You still qualify with good jump."

Jesse started to smile. It made perfect

sense. He could put everything he had into the jump, and not be afraid of fouling. Any decent jump from him would still qualify.

And even better, Jesse realized that his enemy was not an enemy after all. He was just another athlete, wanting to win, but wanting to play fair as well.

Jesse went up for his last qualifying jump. He placed a towel nearly a foot before the takeoff board and walked back to the starting spot. He ran, took off from beside the towel, and shot into the air. His jump of 25 feet, 9 ¾ inches set a new Olympic record. If he hadn't started so far back, he might have broken his own world record. But Jesse didn't care. The important thing was that he had made it into the finals. He had also made a new friend.

In the broad jump finals, Long was Jesse's only serious competitor. The other four finalists were far behind their distances. The time had come for the great battle between American

Jesse Owens and German Lutz Long. But for Jesse, the competition was fun again.

Long jumped first. He matched the old Olympic record. Then Jesse jumped just a little bit farther.

He watched Long's second jump. Long stood as still as a statue, his eyes fixed on a mark in the pit. Then he raced down the runway and took off, flying high above the pit. Jesse thought for a moment that Long would never come down. Finally he landed at 25 feet, 9 ¾ inches. Long had matched the new Olympic record that Jesse had set earlier. The crowd cheered. Jesse rushed over to congratulate Long.

When Jesse's turn came, he stood still at the start of the runway and breathed deeply. He leaned forward and sprinted toward the take-off board. He leaped high, kicking his feet in the air, and landed at 26 feet, ½ inch. He was three inches ahead of Long. Long ran over to shake his hand.

The stadium fell silent as 100,000 spectators watched Long prepare. He had one last chance to gain the lead. He gave it everything he had. But when he landed, he saw the red flag go up. He had stepped over the front edge of the takeoff board. The stadium echoed with groans. Jesse patted Long's shoulder. He felt disappointed, too. Jesse loved a good competition, and this one was over too soon.

Jesse had one jump left, and he had already won. Still, he wasn't going to take it easy. Once again, he would give it his best. On that magical day, he felt like he had wings.

He ran fast, as if sprinting in the 100-meter dash. He hit the takeoff board and leaped into the air. He reached for the clouds.

The Americans in the stands started cheering while Jesse was still in the air. When he started to come back down, he fought against it. He kicked his legs and swung his arms. At last he hit the earth and fell forward. Sand and dirt sprayed up into his face.

Jesse spit out the sand and stood up with a smile. He was sure he had made his best jump ever. Lutz ran over to him. "You did it! I know you did."

They waited as the jump was measured, and the official distance called. Jesse had set a new world record of 26 feet, 5 ¼ inches. Track experts had claimed that no human could ever jump that far. Lutz slapped Jesse on the back while the crowd shouted his name. Jesse and Lutz walked off the field arm in arm.

That evening, Jesse visited Lutz Long at the Olympic Village. They talked for two hours despite Lutz's broken English. They discovered that they actually had a lot in common. Both were from poor backgrounds. Both were twenty-two years old, married, with one child. And of course, both loved sports and worked to be the best. They talked about their worries for the future. What would they do once the Olympics was over? They talked about the racial prejudice in their countries. How would it end? They agreed to write to each other and remain friends, no matter what happened.

Lutz seemed happy with his silver medal. "Don't you care?" Jesse asked. "Aren't you disappointed?"

Lutz said, "I am here to struggle to win. But the one I wish to beat first is always myself."

Jesse nodded. "Then you really did win. You did your best and jumped longer than ever before. And you helped me do my best too." Jesse had found the true meaning of the Olympic spirit.

One Last Race

Jesse woke in the morning and groaned. Two races and six broad jumps had tired out his body. Anger, fear, and joy had exhausted his mind.

"Are you all right?" Coach Snyder asked him.

Jesse managed a smile. "Yesterday was one of the best days of my life. But a day like that takes it out of you."

"I can see that," Snyder said. "But I'm afraid you won't get much rest today."

Jesse sighed and nodded. He had to run the

semifinals and finals in the 200-meter dash. The air was chilly, with dark gray skies overhead. As Jesse boarded the bus, rain started to fall. "Those Germans are a pretty efficient bunch," Jesse joked, "but I guess they don't have the weather in line yet."

The track was muddy, causing trouble for all the morning's events. Pole-vaulters and hurdlers slipped and slid. Still, American athletes won the discus throw and pole vault. The Germans were getting more medals than any other country, but at least Americans were holding their own in track and field.

In the dismal weather, the stadium was only two-thirds full. Jesse tried to take it easy that morning. He kept his sweatshirt on during the semifinals to stay warm. He ran just hard enough to stay in front, and won that race in 21.3 seconds. The best time for any man in the semifinals was 21.1 seconds. That was Mack Robinson, another African American. No German made it to the finals.

The stadium was packed. Everyone wanted to see if Jesse Owens would take home another medal.

Jesse threw off his fatigue and focused on the event ahead. Two gold medals were nice. A third would be even better. This was his last Olympic race—possibly ever. He had to give it everything.

He shot out of the blocks and sped down the track. Once he was moving, it felt easy. He finished in 20.7 seconds, a new Olympic record and a new world record for a curved track. Mack Robinson came in second, a few meters behind him.

The crowd erupted in applause. They knew they were witnessing history.

As Owens and Robinson took the victory stand to get their medals, the drizzle turned into a downpour. Jesse laughed as the fans ran for cover. What did a little rain matter now?

• • •

Finally Jesse got a day of rest. He slept in, then wandered around the Olympic Village. After lunch, he took the bus to the stadium to watch the events. All afternoon people came up to him—other athletes and German spectators. They asked for his autograph and posed with him for pictures. Jesse enjoyed the attention, now that he didn't have to prepare for any more events.

On Saturday morning, August 8, Coach Snyder stuck his head past Jesse's door. "Something's up. Robertson and Cromwell are calling a meeting."

Jesse yawned and scratched his head. Lawson Robertson and Dean Cromwell were two of the official American coaches. Cromwell was in charge of the relay team.

Jesse found the coaches with the men in the 400-meter relay. In the relay, four runners took turns in one race. One man ran 100 meters. He passed a baton to the next man, who ran the next stretch. Relay runners had to be fast. They also had to pass the baton smoothly. If one of them dropped the baton, they would lose the race.

The 400-meter relay runners were Foy Draper, Marty Glickman, Sam Stoller, and Frank Wykoff. They had all run in the 100-meter trials back in the United States. The first three finishers competed in the 100-meter dash, while the next three would join the relay team. Foy, Marty, and Sam had finished fourth, fifth, and sixth. Frank got his spot because he had run the relay at two earlier Olympics.

Jesse wondered why he was in a meeting with the relay team. Ralph Metcalfe was there too, and he raised his eyebrows at Jesse.

Coach Robertson paced in front of the group. He glanced at Sam and Marty, and then away. Finally he cleared his throat and spoke. "We've heard a rumor. The Germans have been saving their best sprinters for the relay. We can't take any chances." He took a deep breath. "We're putting Jesse and Ralph on the team, with Foy and Frank."

For a moment, the room was silent. Then Marty Glickman shot out of his seat. "You can't do that! Sam and I came all the way here just for the relays. We don't have any other events. You can't send us home without even a chance to compete."

Robertson scowled. "We want to win that race, don't we? We're putting our best sprinters in."

"But Foy came in behind us on the last test race," Sam said. "No offense, Foy."

Foy just shook his head. Coach Cromwell said, "Foy and Frank have more experience."

Sam muttered, "Yeah, and it's just a coincidence that they both trained under you back in California."

Marty was still on his feet, waving his hands as he spoke. "Coach, this is ridiculous. The Germans couldn't have hidden world-class sprinters. Runners have to race to get experience. Pick any American relay team you want, and they'll win by fifteen yards. Even our milers or hurdlers could beat the Germans or anyone else by fifteen yards." He shook his head. "Sam and I are the only two Jews on the track team. You keep the two Jews off the team, and there'll be shouting back home."

Robertson said, "Well, we'll see."

Jesse winced at the anger and hurt in the room. This wasn't the Olympic spirit. "Coach, let Sam and Marty run," he said. "I've won three gold medals. That's enough. Give them their chance—they deserve it. Let them run."

Cromwell glared at him. "You'll do what you're told."

Robertson raised his hands as if holding back any more argument. "Look, I'm sorry, but that's the way it is. The decision is made." He walked out of the room, and Cromwell followed.

The runners sat there stunned. Jesse and Ralph muttered their apologies.

"I guess I shouldn't be so surprised," Marty

said. "Cromwell is on the America First Committee. So is Avery Brundage, and he's president of the American Olympic Committee. America First is a pro-Nazi group. I'll bet they just want to save Hitler the embarrassment of seeing Jews on the winners' stand."

"He won't be that happy to see me and Jesse up there again either," Ralph said.

"Yes. Well, have fun." Marty walked out of the room. Sam followed, with one look back at his teammates.

"What do you think?" Jesse asked. "Is there anything in what Marty says?"

Ralph shot a look at Foy and Frank. "More likely in the part that these two are Cromwell's boys. They train with him, so he looks good if they win."

Frank sighed. "I guess it doesn't matter now. It's too late to do anything, with the relay in a few hours."

"I'm sorry for Marty and Sam," Foy said, "but I want to run that race—and win it." He glanced at Jesse. "You can't tell me you won't be happy to get back out there too."

"Sure, I haven't known what to do with myself since Wednesday. And if I'm going to run, I'll sure hustle around that corner. I'm just sorry it had to be like this."

Jesse would run the first leg of the relay. He was glad to go first, since he hadn't practiced passing the baton. By running first, he would start holding the baton and would only have to hand it off to Ralph.

If the Germans had some secret super team, they didn't show up in the morning trials. The Americans matched the world record, forty seconds, with nobody else even close. Still, if Jesse was going to compete at all, he would run his best. It didn't matter how easily they could win, or how many gold medals he already had. Each race was its own reward.

The finals were that afternoon. When the gun went off, Jesse shot forward, running as if it were a 100-meter dash. Ralph started running as Jesse got near him. Jesse held out the baton, still running at top speed. It touched Ralph's hand, then bounced away. Finally Ralph got a firm grip, and Jesse let go. He slowed to a stop as the other teams made their handoffs.

Ralph shot ahead with an astounding burst of speed. By the time he smoothly passed the baton to Foy Draper, they were far ahead of the field. Foy lengthened the lead a bit more, and so did Frank Wykoff. Two of the teams dropped their batons in the last exchange. The Germans ran a smooth race, but never got near the Americans. Frank broke the tape about fifteen yards ahead of them. They set a new world record, finishing in 39.8 seconds.

Jesse joined his teammates, and they headed to the victory stand. Ralph, Foy, and Frank whispered for a minute. "Jesse," Ralph said, "you take the top platform. In honor of your four gold medals."

Jesse smiled. "Gee, thanks! But you don't need to do that." He thought for a moment. "Ralph, you should take that spot. You ran the best of all of us today. You came near to winning a gold medal three times before and had to settle for silver. Now you've finally got your gold."

Ralph grinned, while Foy and Frank nodded their approval.

For a fourth time, Jesse heard America's national anthem played in his honor. With all the trial races, he had competed fourteen times. He came away with four gold medals—more than anyone before in Olympic track history. He set three new world records. He had also shown Hitler—and the world—what a black athlete could do.

Jesse's thoughts went back to Oakville, Alabama. He had started with nothing in his favor, except a decent pair of legs and the love of his family. With hard work, good friends and family, and a little luck, he had become an

Olympic champion. Whatever ups and downs the future held, he had four gold medals to remind him: He was somebody.

In addition to his medals, Jesse went home with four young oak trees, symbols of Olympic growth. The Olympics would keep growing, to include more nations, races, and religions—all competing as equals. To Jesse, the oak trees echoed his own growth. He had grown from a sickly child to a top athlete. He had grown from a poor farm boy to a world-famous hero. His family had grown, to include a wife and child.

He decided to give one of the oaks to his grammar school, one to East Technical High, and one to Ohio State. The last he would save for a house of his own. It would be a memory of his Olympic glory, a glory that would keep growing like a tree, spreading its branches wide.

For More Information

BOOKS

Baker, William J. *Jesse Owens: An American Life*, New York: The Free Press, Macmillan, 1986.

McKissack, Patricia, and Fredrick McKissack. *Jesse Owens: Olympic Star*, Berkeley Heights, NJ: Enslow Publishers, 1992.

Nuwer, Hank. *The Legend of Jesse Owens*, Danbury, CT: Franklin Watts, 1998.

Owens, Jesse, and Paul Neimark. *Jesse: The Man Who Outran Hitler: A Spiritual Autobiography*, Plainfield, NJ: Logos International, 1978.

Owens, Jesse, and Paul Neimark. *The Jesse Owens Story*, New York: GP Putnam's Sons, New York, 1970.

Rennert, Rick. *Jesse Owens: Champion Athlete*, Minneapolis, MN: Tandem Library, 1992.

Streissguth, Tom. *Jesse Owens*, A&E Biography, Minneapolis, MN: Lerner Publications Company, 1999.

Sutcliff, Jane. *Jesse Owens*, Minneapolis, MN: Carolrhoda Books, 2001.

VIDEOS

The Jesse Owens Story, DVD. With Tom Bosley, LeVar Burton, Barry Corbin, and Ronny Cox. Directed by Richard Irving. Quality, 1984.

Olympia I Festival of the Nation, VHS. Directed by Leni Riefenstahl. 1940.

10 Greatest Sports Legends of All Time, VHS. 2000.

This Is Your Life Olympic Champions: Jesse Owens and Duke Kahanamoku, DVD. Hosted by Ralph Edwards. 2006.

WEBSITES

Smithsonian National Museum of American
     History: America on the Move:
          http://americanhistory.si.edu/ONTHEMOVE/

The Jesse Owens Foundation:
     www.jesse-owens.org/about1.html

The Official Jesse Owens website:
     www.jesseowens.com

Official website of the Olympic Movement:
     www.olympic.org

★★★ # Childhood of Famous Americans ★★★

One of the most popular series ever published for young Americans, these classics have been praised alike by parents, teachers, and librarians. With these lively, inspiring, fictionalized biographies—easily read by children of eight and up—today's youngster is swept right into history.

ABIGAIL ADAMS ★ JOHN ADAMS ★ LOUISA MAY ALCOTT ★ SUSAN B. ANTHONY ★ NEIL ARMSTRONG ★ ARTHUR ASHE ★ CRISPUS ATTUCKS ★ CLARA BARTON ★ ELIZABETH BLACKWELL ★ DANIEL BOONE ★ BUFFALO BILL ★ RAY CHARLES ★ ROBERTO CLEMENTE ★ CRAZY HORSE ★ DAVY CROCKETT ★ JOE DIMAGGIO ★ WALT DISNEY ★ AMELIA EARHART ★ DALE EARNHARDT ★ THOMAS EDISON ★ ALBERT EINSTEIN ★ HENRY FORD ★ BEN FRANKLIN ★ LOU GEHRIG ★ GERONIMO ★ ALTHEA GIBSON ★ JOHN GLENN ★ JIM HENSON ★ HARRY HOUDINI ★ LANGSTON HUGHES ★ ANDREW JACKSON ★ MAHALIA JACKSON ★ TOM JEFFERSON ★ HELEN KELLER ★ JOHN FITZGERALD KENNEDY ★ MARTIN LUTHER KING, JR. ★ ROBERT E. LEE ★ MERIWETHER LEWIS ★ ABRAHAM LINCOLN ★ MARY TODD LINCOLN ★ THURGOOD MARSHALL ★ JOHN MUIR ★ ANNIE OAKLEY ★ JACQUELINE KENNEDY ONASSIS ★ ROSA PARKS ★ GEORGE S. PATTON ★ MOLLY PITCHER ★ POCAHONTAS ★ RONALD REAGAN ★ CHRISTOPHER REEVE ★ PAUL REVERE ★ JACKIE ROBINSON ★ KNUTE ROCKNE ★ MR. ROGERS ★ ELEANOR ROOSEVELT ★ FRANKLIN DELANO ROOSEVELT ★ TEDDY ROOSEVELT ★ BETSY ROSS ★ WILMA RUDOLPH ★ BABE RUTH ★ SACAGAWEA ★ SITTING BULL ★ DR. SEUSS ★ JIM THORPE ★ HARRY S. TRUMAN ★ SOJOURNER TRUTH ★ HARRIET TUBMAN ★ MARK TWAIN ★ GEORGE WASHINGTON ★ MARTHA WASHINGTON ★ LAURA INGALLS WILDER ★ WILBUR AND ORVILLE WRIGHT

★★★ # Collect them all! ★★★